THRIVERS

An LP Novel

Franco Book 2 of 3
*Also reads as a
Stand-Alone Story

Tom Sheridan

Streets Creations

Published in the United States by Streets Creations.

ISBN-10: 1-7321758-2-9
ISBN-13: 978-1-7321758-2-2

To Tamara
I howl this song for you

And for good wolves
everywhere

TRACKS

TRACK 1. MINUTES TO MIDNIGHT

TJ STOOD ON A LEDGE. At Jersey's northeastern edge. Hours after sunset. Franco the Fighter's son set. To leap to his permanent sunset.

Cuz no matter how long T lived. He'd be haunted by The Thing. That unerasable stain. That cancer on his brain. That cavity in his heart. Fuck. It infected every part. From the stress in the back of his neck. To his tingling toes on the ledge of the deck. Hanging ten on the concrete giant like Laird Hamilton. Across from Broadway lit up with *Hamilton*. About all T could see. Through the rain. Beneath the fog.

Meanwhile his father. Was he even bothered? Probably at his fight club back in The Wood. Pretendin it's all good.

While the monkey grew on T's back. Now deformed and black. A demon. T could see him. Over his shoulder havin a good chuckle. As T's knees buckled...

The college senior with an internship on Wall. Fraternity brother who'd rock the mic on call. But after the show. The low. An insomniac in his bedroom dark. Listening to Linkin Park. Usually *Minutes to Midnight*. For the kid. Minutes to midnight.

But as TJ stood on the ledge. It was his own lines haunting his head–

Sick as my secret
Just wanna secrete it
Drag it out beat it
But it's undefeated

TJ heard it over and over. At least it was about to be. *Game Over.* Soon as T. Counted to three. He could do anything after a three count. Like when he'd asked Kamara out.

One. The wind howled. Like God was an owl. *Fwooooh...*

Two. The rain soaked Hoboken. Pelted T as he bent his knees. *Fwooooh...*

Thr–

TRACK 2. FRANCO 2.0

"YOU HEAR WHAT BASAYEV TWEETED?" Joey Yo asked Franco.

"I only hear birds tweet."

Franco hadn't been on social media since seven years before. Since the fall of '08. Since The Thing. *Coincidence,* concluded Woodbridge's Bunns Lane Brawler. He was busy back then. He'd just retired. Just bought a house out in Branchton. Gave Julie the dream house she always wanted. Okay, the one *he* always wanted to give her. Thought it was the right move for teen T too. Better school n all that. And definitely the right move for number two. T's little sister. Franco wanted to name her Kimberly after his late foster mother. Julie wanted to name her Sydney after the city she never got to study abroad in. They compromised on Kyd. *It's got Woodbridge roots. Everyone calls each other kid,* Franco would kid. *What's good, kid? How you been, kid? How's your kid, kiiid?*

Franco drove as Joey's voice droned over the Dodge Charger's speakers...

"He Tweeted, 'Randy Couture was a champ at 46. Franco couldn't even make 36.'"

"Too bad I don't have the steroids Basayev has."

"What ah stewoids?" asked the almond-eyed girl from her booster seat. The week before she was born at the end of '08, Franco moseyed his Mustang into the dealership. Turned in two doors for four. Thought he'd go with blue again. But at the last minute, went as gray as his temples.

"Steroids are drugs that help your body in the short run... then crush it in the long run."

"Hey Kyd," began Uncle Joey by way of Bluetooth. "Tell your Uber driver I'll catch him at the gym."

"My daddy doesn't dwive Ubuh," snickered the six-year-old still trying to master her r's.

"Might be soon..."

"Yeah yeah see you soon."

Franco refocused on the rural road. Kept a look out for darting deer. Then fawned over his own fawn in the rearview... "I say Derek Jeter, you say..."

"Bawwwing."

"K. How bout... I say Elsa, you say..."

Snores from Kyd.

"Your brother used to play this game with me all the time. Answer's only gotta be three words or less—"

Kyd snored louder.

"Alright. What do *you* wanna talk about?"

"How do they make electwicity?"

Back in the day, when little TJ asked these questions, Franco would just tell him to ask his mother. Or his teacher. Now? In 2015? Franco had to pull the car over. Type into his phone's web browser: *how do they make electricity.*

Five minutes and five follow-up questions later, Franco was back on the road.

And in five more, pulling up to an expansive clearing. Anchored by an elementary school. Coconut concrete striped

4

with tinted windows. Solar-paneled canopies topping the parking lot.

Franco glanced the SUVs ahead of him in the drop-off line. Audi. Buick. Cadillac. A. B. C. Followed by his Dodge. Fuckin Franco. Forty-one and still gettin Ds at school.

Kyd unbuckled and grabbed her backpack. "We're luhning subtwaction today. It's when you staht with one numbah. Then take away fwom it."

"K don't forget your speech homework. In the small pocket—"

Kyd slammed her door and bopped off—

"Ay!"

Kyd turned. "I huhd you!"

"Not that..."

"Oh. Yeah..."

Kyd brushed her sandy waves out of the way. Dished a daily wink with her missing front teeth.

Franco returned a wink with his capped canine.

"You stay-at-home dads don't get enough credit."

Franco's attention crossed to the crossing guard— "Me? No. I'm Franco."

"I didn't know Francos were outlawed from being stay-at-home fathers," huffed the hefty lady.

I'm Franco. That statement went pretty far in the wake of the championship win. *March of '08. Man was everything great.* "I mean, uh, I own a gym. Have a good one." Franco stepped on the gas.

The crossing guard watched the unartful Dodge eat it on a speed bump. *"I'm Franco.'* Huh. I'm Nancy."

The Charger tore down 287. Roared south past South Plainfield as Franco's imagination wandered toward the high school. The one boasting the best wrestling squad in the state. What if Franco had went to school with those guys? Squared-away kids from a squared-away town. Disciplined kids that won districts and D-1 scholarships. Then shipped out into the world shipshape.

The Dodge meanwhile pressed toward Woodbridge aka The Wood. The town where Franco played basketball instead. Took gravity hits to the head. In eighth grade. By ninth, got laid. By tenth, wanted to be mafia made. Who needed good grades? He ran dice *and* spades. Chasing shorties, drinkin 40s. Living like he'd never see his 40s.

Well, here they were. Franco checked his look in the rearview. And saw the present. Forty-one years' worth of creases in his forehead. Crows' feet crawling out his eyes. Pock marks pecking his face.

But. His left arm stretched to the helm. Ripped. Thank God for the fight game. The health habits Franco had built had stuck. Three whole-food meals a day. And the training with his up-and-coming fighter. His feet had never felt lighter.

Franco switched arms at the helm as his thoughts switched to coaching. What if it was tunnel vision? Banking on his new sensation. To turn his club into a magnet destination. For the best fighters in the nation. Like how Bobby Brazil had done for his Jiu-Jitsu gym. Yeah Franco was right behind him...

In a Dodge. Trapped in traffic. Crawling across tracks. Their lining woods a reminder of The Thing. As if Franco wasn't already thinkin about enough things. The fuckin Thing. Seven years and still lingering. Sure, it happened out in Branchton. But the wood-lined tracks were a reminder. Franco's head craning... His foot on the gas...

Then on the brakes– SCREECH–

Almost rear-ending the car in front of him–

Its driver welcoming the former world champ home,

"Asshole!"

Woodbridge. The great meritocracy. The town that told Franco he was great in '08. And. Just another asshole in '15.

Franco trucked onto the rugged stretch of road where Route 1 merged with 9 to become US 1 & 9. Like neither highway wanted to take full credit for the flea bag motels. The shoddy auto bodies. The brick-faced fight club. The one with the sign above it: *Brawlers.* Named after The Bunns Lane Brawler himself. A name chosen by... who else? The one-hit wonder himself.

Franco looked to the roof of the fight club. *Damn.* Just last summer, he'd sit up there with his Bud Lights on Friday nights. Stare at the Freedom Tower. Fancy his son a world power. His... intern son. Still interning. And their Blue-Collar Scholars charity? Relying on charity. T's fraternity. Him and other brothers helping disadvantaged kids from The Wood out. But what happens... when the senior's time runs out?

The Dodge rolled over gravel popping like popcorn. Franco parked it next to Julie's hybrid. Julie aka gym manager aka hostess aka bookkeeper. There since 7:00 am. In early to be out early to pick up Kyd. Franco meanwhile in late to stay late for another kid. His up-and-comer.

Franco checked his car's clock: 9:09. Like it was Ecclesiastes 9:9. *Enjoy life with your wife, whom you love... For this is your lot in life and in your toilsome labor under the sun.*

Franco'd never read the Bible in a million years. He'd haveth no ideath what it sayeth. But as the fighter floundered through life once again, he'd looked to his role models once again. (Nah not Stifler n Paul Rudd.) Coach Nelson and Bobby Brazil. One raised proper in Woodbridge Proper. The other on the same block as The Bunns Lane Brawler. One white. One black. Two "opposites" from Woodbridge. Faith their common bridge. So Franco started browsing biblehub.

7

Started peekin on Wikipedia. Pickin up tidbits. Not that the Catholic church didn't give him fits. Them and *their* fuckin Thing–

The glass door's bell ring–

Snapped Franco out of it–

He took a breath and continued into Brawlers. Usually spent the first hour mingling with the mixed martial artists. Shook hands at the heavy bags. Joked with coach Joey. Gave pointers to semi-pros tangling with Taz.

First hour was a rough estimate. *First hour* was the entire morning back in '08. Back when the sight of Franco, let alone a handshake or a shout, was enough to make a member's year. Now, in '15? The membership totaled 15. A couple of them in there at any given time. Getting his or her own private lesson at plebeian prices. Franco was now making his rounds in 15 minutes. *Fifteen minutes of fame...*

Followed by a walk of shame. Into the back office of backed-up paperwork. Julie toiling away, trying to make it all work. With the same computer, phone, and throne installed seven years prior. Locked in time like a set by Richard Pryor.

Julie herself, meanwhile, had made a couple adjustments. The glasses she started wearing six years earlier. As if she'd put them on for one long look at the way the gym was headed. While the paperwork and supplies kept piling the other way. Her other change was her *cup a' cawfee*. Used to be a tall latte from Starbucks. Now? Dunkin' Donuts. A Joe Blow cup of jo. At least it was double the size. Like the mounting supplies...

Julie did her best to organize it all in the space so small. Even had shelves installed. Shelves overflowing with headgear out the rear. As stacked boxing glove boxes boxed the room in further yet. And the coat tree of Jiu-Jitsu gis? About to topple like that board game Topple.

Captain Julie. Keeping the *SS Franco* afloat as long as possible. Eleven more years would be nice. Until Kyd was off to college. More like 11 more weeks. End of the current lease. The ship about to wreck as Julie's speaker played "Ship to Wreck."

Franco's favorite move was to pop in, observe the overloaded room and say, *Ay we could probably open another store with all this stuff.* Pretend the rocks glass with the half shot left in it was half full. Take the sting out of the inevitable notes about membership sinking. Overdue dues rising. *We juicin em?* Franco would joke. Then he'd get lost in the weeds on Julie's explanations of operating cash flow (or lack thereof). Followed by the relationship between assets, liabilities, and (negative) shareholder equality. Or was it equity? And what was the difference? "You connect with Lama?"

Lama. Franco's manager. The one who'd mined his nugget of fortune n fame. She'd set up spots all over the state. Appearances at bars on fight nights. Car dealer commercials. Franco even did elbow rubs at country clubs. Spoke at events for dudes with so much money... it wasn't funny. But every year since the fighter retired from MMA... they all had less and less to pay. Franco. A fallen king of NJ.

All the while, the Branchton house and Brawlers bills just kept coming. Like Jersey Shore waves when it's humming. And how big were his son's student loans? Franco didn't even wanna know...

Julie's answer not much better. "A win this weekend? We'll see a little something."

"They still don't wanna ink? Kid's been on fire."

"Minor leagues. They need to see a win for The Show."

Franco leaned on the doorway. His hazels gazing into Jewels' blues. A fleeting respite from his blues. "Better get to it then."

Franco segued to the next part of his day. His grueling workouts that made sure he could give the kid one. Push-ups. Pull-ups. Jump rope. Squat rack.

Then over to the cage. More prep for the up-and-comer who'd tangled with a Tonio Franco back in the day. Tonio Franco *Junior.* TJ.

Ray. The schoolyard brawler now at Brawlers. Now 23 and working on his game for the past five years. His big shot—Coach Franco's big shot, the whole gym's big shot—now five *days* away. Ray's first fight for The Show. On their monthly Saturday Night Fights card. This one down in AC.[1] The opponent from overseas. A Judo black belt. An understudy of Umar "The Beast" Basayev. The Black Sea bomber who'd handed Franco his last loss back in the day. One punishing punch at a time.

After another pad Thai lunch from Taz's—save for Franco, his health habits as sticky as his brown rice—the fight team readied for the sparring session with Ray.

The jacked Joey straightened his headgear. Grabbed his sparring shield. Entered the cage like it was the Colosseum.

Franco entered behind him. Gloves and headgear of his own. "Warm me up before the kid?"

Joey threw his padded shield aside. Danced around the canvas with Franco...

"So what about Basayev? He's gonna be in AC."

"So what."

"So that Tweet. He's startin shit," jabbed Joey.

"So?" Franco parried.

"So we gotta be ready." Joey threw a hook.

Franco dodged. "Take it easy."

---

[1] As in Atlantic City. Not as in air condition or nothin. Or that alternatin current Kyd had him lookin up.

"If I wanted to hit ya, I'd hit ya."

"Only thing we gotta be ready for is a W."

"Amen," noted Nelly. The 48-year-old Athletic Director's hairline as wound down as his career. Eyes as emerald as ever, though. The wrestling coach clawing the cage as...

Taz pulled up next to him. The undersized Muay Thai coach with an undercut to his chin. "Ray already gets a W every day. Kicking Franco's ass."

"It's called a sparring *partner,*" defended Franco.

"And you can bet Aram has been goin at it with The Beast," gnawed Nelly.

"Our kid moves, not to mention looks, a hell of a lot better than The Beast." Franco motioned toward the lockers...

The kid's size 15 feet made their way. Topped by oversized ankles. Long shins loaded with calf muscle. Disney turkey legs elongated. Softball-sized knees. Quads that popped forward as much as his backside popped back. From wide hips harboring a tornado-shaped torso. A tornado spiraling out into broad shoulders that swayed with confidence. The kid a moving tree. Six-three. Struttin like Kyrie. After six threes. As his fade blended up. From a one to a two to a three. As he clocked the hope in the eyes of Franco, Taz, Joey. Even Nelly. Julie.

And as Ray entered the cage...

Coach Franco's mind drifted to the upcoming Saturday night. The end of the fight. His star's hand goes up. The whole place erupts.

Or.

The Franco gym goes bankrupt.

TRACK 3. TJ ALL DAY

"KEEP YOUR FEET SIDEWAYS TO THE NET,"
instructed TJ.

Kyd shot her feet sideways. Then forward. Then
sideways. Then forward. The six-year-old with the racquet
causing a racket. Her demeanor as colorful as her activewear's
pink, purple, and teal. Big brother meanwhile in black from
head to heel.

She had good footwork, he had to admit. Now if she could
actually stand still... "Like I showed you." TJ, in front of the
net, demonstrated once more in slow-motion. Brought his
racquet back. Came through low, open-faced. Turned the
racquet over on the follow-through.

Kyd did the same. At lightning speed.

But even in the blink of an eye, T could tell she'd swung
right. *The blink of an eye.* One second you're walking along the
tracks on a beautiful fall day. The next you cut into the
woods. And it's suddenly gray. You're suddenly watching
sunrises from the crack in your shades. Sleepless night after
sleepless night. After hours of demon fights. TJ getting up.
Saying he was aight. To spare all the despair. Many places

since. His head always there–

"Excuse me, mistuh."

What– who–– oh T's sister. Looking up at the mind drifter... "I swung my wacquet like a million billion times." Kyd added a few more for good measure. "Thwow one aweady."

TJ smiled wide over her tiny mouth. The one causing the speech impediment along with her long tongue. Not that it ever stopped the little one. "Okay. Get ready."

Kyd turned sideways. Her tight shirt popped by her pot belly. The little squirt about to growth spurt.

TJ bounced a ball her way.

Kyd got the first part of the swing right–popped it sky high.

TJ re-demonstrated the over-the-top follow-through.

Kyd popped another one sky high.

"Do you see a net up there?"

"That cloud looks like a net."

TJ motioned his racquet to the net next to him. "This one's easier to reach."

"Not if yuh God."

TJ laughed. Looked to the heavens clustered with cumulonimbus. "Maybe if you practice more, you can play him one day."

"What if God's a guhl?"

TJ paused his ball bouncing. What he had assumed. Or had been told. Either way. On the possibility sold. As he looked at the six-year-old. "Then maybe you can play her one day. Come on, follow through."

TJ bounced Kyd another one.

Her line drive skimmed his hair–

Big bro sold his shock with wide eyes–

Kyd doubled over laughing. "Sahwee!"

"That was perfect! But. I'm still gonna get ya." TJ chased Kyd as she shrieked with laughter...

"I didn't do it on puhpose!"

TJ helped the six-year-old out of his seven-year-old car. A used black Mustang. One he bought after working all of the prior summer. Seven days a week. Around the clock save for sleeping and commuting. And the occasional rager. Ostensibly to unwind. But they only made things worse.

TJ left the kindergartner on her late-start Friday the same way Franco would leave him back in the day. By pointing to his own chest. Then hers. His own. Then hers.

Kyd did the same at rapid-fire pace and ran off.

Franco and Julie had acted like TJ was doing them a big favor. Taking Kyd to play tennis then dropping her off for half-day Fridays. But watching his little sister run off with her backpack bobbing—*actually excited about where she was going*—was the best part of his day. His week. His life.

TJ tore through Branchton's winding, wooded roads. Concerns more near and dear than deer. More near and dear than what TJ usually did on these roads. Curse that the family ever moved there. The Woodbridge boy bounced to Branchton for his final three years of high school. Went from being cool to some nobody fool. But on that day, that's not what his head was going over. As it pounded from his hangover. Returning hours after his morning coffee n ibuprofen back in Hoboken. The town the college senior was now returning to as his memory of the prior night also returned. Yeah the girl was nice. But commitment? Too high a price. TJ had been through that sham before. A high school summer with Lenore. Swearing their love forevermore. The following summer no more. She smushing Ray down the

15

shore. TJ quothing the Raven. *Nevermore!*

The fan of Edgar Allan poetry shifted in his seat. Shifted the Stang into overdrive. Steppin on the gas to make that pain-in-the-ass class. Which would be followed by a ferry to The City for some never-ending interning. A full-time job offer, or lack thereof, dangling in front of T like a carrot he'd been walking toward all of senior year. Dangling by a thread like his dad's fight club. The one that had motivated TJ to major in business in the first place.

Before it had opened, teen T's mind had wandered from this potential future to that. Maybe a psychologist? Nah they were all quacks. Generations of Francos knew that. Like Franco's foster father. Left Vietnam and never looked back. Oh and that psychologist Julie's sister married. An eccentric with three degrees and all of two patients. After all the school and all the payments. *Dad's last fight fortune.* Blew it faster than a hick hittin the lottery. Down payments (and debts) on a new house. A risky business. Of course T was gonna major in business. End the Francos' never-ending loop of going broke. What a joke. So forget T's other idea of becoming a teacher. Undergrad *and* grad school to come out makin $50K a year. But have no fear, the student loans only last ten years. By then, Kyd'll be in a project on Bunns Lane. No. Way.

The driving kid all in a stew was even gonna wrap the rap game too. Yeah his audience had grown. But so did the number of wannabe rappers. It was only him, everyone, and their mother on AudioCloud. T was just another face in the crowd. Yeah maybe down the road he could stand out. But he couldn't wait for that to play out. He had to bail his family out. He was gonna work on Wall Street. No. Doubt.

TJ took a deep breath on the rust-belt highway. Up ahead: the Pulaski Skyway. The black expanse slithering over the swamps of Jersey like a mega-viper making its way to

Manhattan. T's hands on the wheel suddenly swampier than that surrounding marshland. His heart pumping like the behemoth bridge pumping cars. *All it takes is a turn of the wheel...*

T's feet sweating...

His body steaming...

Over the sight of the demon. Piled in the passenger seat. Cranium craned against the roof. The dark figure glistening of goo.

TJ's hands squeezing the wheel at ten-and-two. A simple yank would do... Like that saying. Cut off your nose to spite... *the demon in your passenger seat...*

TJ's shaking hand popped the center console.

The car zigged as—

The driver popped a bottle. Popped a pill. Stuck it under his tongue. Rubbed it into his gum.

But the ride... *wasn't even close to done...*

The Mustang was *still* elevating.

TJ's point of view as skyward as an astronaut headed for orbit. An astronaut launched unwillingly. *Calm down T, don't be silly.*

Thousands of people drive over this bridge everyday. TJ tried to look their way... but looking at everyone else included a look into the great wide open. T ironically hearing "Into The Great Wide Open." *The impact from this height is like hitting a brick wall. Are you ready to take that fall?*

"Agghhh!" screamed T. *Like he did that day running through the sticks. Seven years later and still sick—*

TJ's hands now *twisting* the wheel at ten-and-two... A simple yank would do... *Don't look up. Don't look left. And definitely don't look right. Forget him, alright!* Just focus on the road right in front of you. Yeah just look... down. *And calm down. Chill... Wait for that pill...*

17

The prospect of future peace...
Was enough for the Mustang to cross in one piece.

Shit, the Clonium even had T feeling *good* as he approached his hood. He'd made it through the dark parts of *The Marshall Mathers LP 2* and was now cutting loose with "Love Game." About how relationships were insane.

The Mustang paralleled into a spot. In front of an abandoned lot.

TJ was so far out on the square-mile town's edge, he was able to slap a *"Welcome to Hoboken: Birthplace of Baseball and Frank Sinatra"* sign on his way. Hearing Frank's "A Foggy Day."

Old brownstones turned to new condos as T's sneaks snuck into upper-class confines. Then soldiered on. Toward the hill on the Hudson...

Jersey State University at Hoboken. JSUH. The crown jewel of Jersey education. *Public* Jersey education. The real princes were down at Princeton. JSUH did have the look of Princeton. Just half the size. And a hundredth the endowment. Students who didn't know what the Dow meant. That was TJ's glass half-full reminder as he walked through the gates of his historic Jersey college. Yeah Wall Street wasn't banging down JSUH's door, but the competition in the classroom wasn't as intense either.

Until lately. The banker boy was in such a rush to build his résumé that he'd finished his finance concentration in three years. Senior year was for finishing his minor: "Societal Studies." A hybrid of social sciences classes. A few years ago, the fresh-faced frosh had made it his minor for a simple reason: it sounded interesting. And for the most part, TJ enjoyed it. But his upcoming class, he'd void it.

TJ cut through students fidgeting with iPhones and vape pens. On the campus walled off like a state pen. Most of the haunts a hundred years old. Some a few hundred. All as gray as the day. The sunshine left behind like Kyd had taken it with her.

TJ now among Gothic buildings looking out at Gotham. Headed for the grandest of them all. Hudson Hall. Towering over oaks barren like fall. The trees breaking spring rules. Playing April Fools'.

But as TJ made his way on the dim day, he saw the light...

The girl with the golden eyes. More gold in her highlights. Shooting across her dark curls like fireworks in the night. Those bushy curls that popped high above her top. A tank that tankfully exposed her singular skin tone. *Caramel.* Like that girl that sings "Caramel." The flannel around her waist flowing. Her skin glowing. Kamara Day. An aura for days.

T in a daze...

The two about to merge...

Until Kamara's petite pal pushed past him—

Sori. Another story.

One that began on the first day of the spring "Contemporary Culture" class.

"How about you, doggie?" asked the professor with short hair and bangs draping her face like stage curtains. Her focus on T. On the print on his T...

"Oh. Our fraternity. Delta. Omega. Gamma."

"But you all do go by, 'Dog?'"

"Yeah I guess..."

"You guess? It's on the banner hanging on your house."

The banner. Hanging well past rush week. Well past the objections of T. The house VP. Not that T could divulge

19

those details. The president was sitting right next to him. The two sitting at one of four Formica tables in the form of a square.

Dr. Goa grilling from the left. Staring. Glaring. The room reflecting off her Kanda glasses... "I know the signs in here might not be as appealing. But if you had to pick one to say something about..."

TJ looked around the room reminiscent of his freshman year of high school. His last in Woodbridge. Cinderblock walls. Gray gloss paint. Wood-glass door. The throwback classroom even had the contemporary faces. Ones as diverse as a UN meeting. Only difference was, this room had social messages and posters hung about. The ones Dr. Goa was talking about... TJ's turn to pick one out...

"I like that one."

TJ pointed to a print: A full-figured nude woman posing on a day bed. With a gorilla mask over her head. Captioned: *¿Tienen que estar desnudas las mujeres para entrar en el Met?* The subcaption further noted that less than four percent of artists on display at the Met were wome–

"Of course the frat boy picks the one with the naked 'chick'," seared Sori. Fuming like a bull with her black nose ring.

As classmates piled on with supporting *mm hmms*.

"I mean... it's a good message." TJ translated the Spanish part, "It says, *Do women have to be nude to get into the Met?* Meaning, why not as artists? Women are at least as artistic as men–"

"What do you mean *at least?*" grilled Sori. Her auburn eyes burning a hole in T.

"I don't know... art is based on emotio..."

"Oh so women are more emotional than men. Thanks for mansplaining that."

"Manwhat?"

"Doesn't even know he's doing it," added Anders, Sori's ally to her left.

TJ's eyes toggled between the coed classmates. Then over to Dr. Goa...

Her exquisite eyebrows raised above her glasses. As if to say, *Maybe they're right...*

And what about the girl to Sori's right...

Kamara Day. What did her look say?

Hard to say for TJ. As the semester wore on, Kamara tended to agree more with Sori than the unabashed ally to T's right. The DOG house president who, on that first day, came in hotter than a fighter plane into enemy territory–

"First of all. She's not even hot," fired Gary aka G. His brushed hair faded down to a three. His long forearms sprouting from rolled-up sleeves. His comment causing the proverbial record scratch. Causing the non-verbial looks of– *Oh no he just didn't!*

Dr. Goa took her glasses off. She was gonna handle this one herself. *"Hotness* is a social construct. In fact, heavyset women in that nude model's time *were* considered attractive."

"Okay fine. But it's 2015. And if we're being honest, my friend T here wouldn't be attracted to her."

All eyes on T. *Jee, thanks G!* If T could crawl under the table, he would. Dig a tunnel back to The Wood. Back to childhood...

"Why wouldn't you be attracted to her?" asked the professor of a similar figure.

"I... didn't say that..." shrugged T.

"Because the patriarchy has constructed the ideal woman to be thin. To keep them *weak*," concluded Sori. As she stared down T!

TJ wanted to point out that his ideal woman was the one

next to Sori. With the thick thighs and shoulders pitch perfect. Boss as those girls in *Pitch Perfect*. But there was probably something fucked up about that too! About everything T knew! "I... don't even know what the patriarchy is," admitted the business major.

"Well a fish doesn't know it's in water," Sori clapped back. As the class clapped that. As Dr. Goa sat back. As if to say, *And that's that.*

Now it was April first. And G was about to burst. His dark eyes scowling. Like a character from Rowling. Watching as...

Dr. Goa rose with papers pressed against her chest. Like a CIA analyst toting top-secret information. "You may take a *private* look at your grade. Then please put your paper away."

Dr. Goa made it around the horn to T. It was a B. Hopefully it didn't matter. Hopefully the spring senior would have a job offer before final grades. But it might matter. He raised his hand to ask if this paper, like prior ones, would have a re-submission—

And was beaten into submission—

"Privilege check!" charged Sori.

"Not today, heteronormative white boy," insulted Anders—the boy of paler complexion than T.

Heterowhat? wondered the "white" boy. If race was a social construct, then T and his hair shaped to a point up front and paled skin from the last two years indoors... was white. His orphan father's ethnicity be damned. Franco's ethnicity that may have been unearthed. By a fan that came out of the woodwork. After the '08 fight in Newark. A 90-year-old nurse. Saying she was there at birth. An immigrant mother from Brazil. Who said the father was a local. *Newark and Brazil.* That only covered every ethnicity! And what did it even matter, jeez!

Mattered right then to T. He almost forgot. It was a day of silence in the classroom for those of *privilege*. Read: G and T. T the kid with the orphan father from the projects. And the mom who single-mommed it for half his childhood. Takin down ten bucks an hour at Jersey Power.

"Bullsh–" G's sh–

Turned into a *"SHOOSH!"* by the class turned Greek chorus.

G slammed his paper on the table–

The Greek chorus gasped–

Then covered some laughs– At the site of his grade–

F.

"An F is still better than a G," Sori whispered to Kamara.

TJ stretched his neck for a glance at the title but lost it in the glare. He'd have to ask G back at the house. G who, right then, was opening his outlawed mouth–

"You *picked* today as the day of silence so you can hand me this paper without discussion."

Anders made the shh sign. "Save the hot air for the frat house."

"My fraternity house has more diversity than this groupthink class. We have all kinds of brothers–"

"Oh yeah?" inquired Sori. "Are any of them *women?*"

Ooohs from the Greek chorus.

"Mic drop," added Anders.

G looked to Dr. Goa...

"Sori makes an interesting point."

G stood up. Stormed away with his leather satchel like he was Satchel Paige. *Maybe by 42, G would be welcome too!* The thought reminded G of *his* favorite poster. The one he stood under at the door. "Didn't MLK say, judge not by the color of one's–"

"SHOOSH!"

With that, kid took off. Like a Nike Swoosh.

TJ meanwhile glanced to Kamara. Their eyes met for an awkward beat. Then beat it in opposite directions...

When class ended, TJ herded out, overheard Kamara and Sori...

"Are you coming to Wall Wall Street?"

"I have to meet my thesis advisor. Tomorrow though," countered Kamara.

TJ continued out of Hudson Hall. Crossed the outdoor mall. Usually, he left with G. *So was this an opportunity?* To ask Kamara out... His mind flooded with doubt. *Lenore. He was done with girlfriends, he swore!* Not to mention the butterflies that fluttered. What if he stuttered? And what the... *T was usually a cool customer with the ladies.* Oh but this one. *Was a Mercedes.* And it was the anticipation that ate him alive, wasn't it? At least if he went for it, it would all be over. One way or the other. So T followed his rule of three. Once he counted to three, he could do anything so long as it didn't hurt anyone else...

One.

Two.

Three.

"Hey. Excuse me—"

"We're busy!" shouted Sori as she hauled across the mall—

But Kamara had stopped. *Even turned toward T...*

"Hi," T said with a little smile and wave.

"Hi," Kamara mimicked.

"Well, what is it?" asked a returning Sori.

"My paper? An A..." Kamara flashed it to TJ. "Your peer edits were awesome. And funny."

TJ smiled. "Sorry for any tangents."

"Your little sister sounds cute." Kamara motioned toward his backpack. "I'm sure you got an A too..."

"Ah, B actually."

"Really?" Kamara wrinkled her brow.

"Your edits were bomb, though."

"Now that that's all settled..." Sori clutched Kamara's arm to yank her away–

But she stayed. *What did this boy want to say?...*

"I was actually wondering... if you wanted to hang out tonight."

"What time?"

"What time's good for you?"

"Eight?"

"Eight is great," agreed T.

"It's also crazy."

"K it's a date. At crazy eight," said T with a smile.

"It'll be crazy or great," concluded Kamara.

Sori rolled her eyes and rolled away.

Not that TJ noticed. His eyes were on another set of eyes. Cuz even on a gray day. They were golden all the way.

TRACK 4. RAY OF HOPE

ONE HAD A CHAIN. ONE HAD A PIPE. ONE HAD A BAT. As all three attacked. The batter with the eyebrow ring took the first swing. Ray learned a long time ago to parry to the right of a righty. It was against the swinger's momentum. And as the bat passed left, Ray unloaded a left. A cross that rattled the dude's cross. Made Jesus jump. While the one with the pipe took a swipe. But Ray absorbed it like Bounty– Wrangled it like a Mountie– All while robbin the bat man. The senior's high school aide should've seen Ray then. He was multitasking!

But if two's company, three's that third fucker chokin you with a chain. Pulling on it like the drawstrings of a trash bag. A trash bag his trailer trash homies helped him trash...

The three dragged the immobile kid from the mobile homes. Stomped toward the swamp. Asking the kid from the trailer homes, *You ready to die homes?* Ray writhed and twisted. Like a Florida gator that didn't appreciate being relocated to a Jersey swamp. But the chain man only pulled harder. Tilted Ray toward some final rays.

Franco preferred taking back roads outta Woodbridge. Route 1 was a nightmare. Both the traffic and the chewed-up roads. So Franco traded potholes for podcasts. *The Breakfast Club* for breakfast. Afternoons, he'd take his mind off the club's bills by listening to the Bills. Burr n Simmons.[2]

And back on that day in 2010, as he listened to a pod, he pondered a sign. The one on the trailer park he passed: "Quality Homes." And Franco figured... it was kinda true! Shit, the king of Rome would pawn his palace for AC n TV.[3] Why couldn't the Francos just live there? Oh cuz it's all relative ain't it? Other people got more, more, more. So you gotta score, score, score. Franco thought he'd beat the video game of life back in '08. But there's always a next floor, floor, floor. What a rat race. Someone just drag Franco into the marsh. Like that poor mahfucka— Wait—

The sun was ablaze as Ray looked up at those rays. The kid writhing. Raising all the hell he could raise.

Ray managed to boot away one of the ushers with footwork worthy of Usher. Was even able to rise for a beat. Flail fists and feet. Every which way without precision. Till he was choked. Back to limbo position. Still, Ray writhed. On a mission...

And whadayaknow— The stranglehold came undone— The three bangers went on the run—

"Ay what the fuck is goin on here!" shouted the OG charging like a bull...

---

[2] And yeah yeah, Julie had to set up the car's Smarttooth or whatever it's called.

[3] Oh they're called emperors ain't they? *Come on Franco.*

"That's Franco yo!"

"Go!"

Franco rolled up to the rolled-up kid. Ha. More like man-child. Young buck was bigger than Franco. "You okay?"

"I had them bruh" doubled down the doubled-over kid.

Bruh? Franco was twice this kid's age! And had been in a fuckton more fights. But if Franco, *The Bunns Lane Brawler*, was bein honest? He appreciated the moxie from the kid who coulda took two of em. Shit, without weapons, he woulda whooped all three. With his four-star frame. Franco's mind already in fifth gear... "You ever been trained to fight?"

"Yeah right here." Ray motioned his albatross arm at the trailer park at-large.

"Quality Homes, huh?" joked Franco.

"They have air conditioning, don't they?" snapped Ray.

Mother– Franco jogged after the kid. Tucked his aviators in the rear of his t-shirt collar. A trick he'd picked up from years of picking up his kids. The shades dropped from the front too many times. "Yeah no you're right. TV too. I mean, what else ya want, right?"

"To be left alone bruh." Ray hurried off. Technically, he strutted off. But with his long stride, Franco had to jog to keep up. Took note of the stray's Strahan jersey...

"Right. Right. Strahan didn't need no one either."

The comment stopped the kid in his tracks. "Nigga what?"

"Nothin except a coach. A team. A field."

"A dentist," added Ray. Then off Franco's look– "You don't know him, do you? Don't tell him I said that."

"Sure he could get it fixed if he wanted." Franco exhaled a chuckle. "But it adds character."

Ray wrinkled his brow over the insight...

"Anyway how bout you? You wanna talk about gaps?"

29

You got big gaps in your technique," tallied Franco.

"Man what are you sayin?"

"Don't take a genius to watch a minute of Strahan and know he's next-level."

"So you wanna come smoke purp. Watch Strahan highlights?"

"I'm sayin. I grew up fightin on these streets too. The eye test don't lie."

"Okay I'll YouTube some Kimbo Slice. Make a couple bucks bare knuckling." Ray ascended his aluminum steps. All three in a single step.

"Ay. Hold up."

"Can't you read the sign?"

Ray nodded to the handwritten sign taped on the trailer: NO SOLICITERS.

"Solicitors are sellin something. I'm sayin, come to my gym... *for free.*"

"Man, get the fuck outta here."

Normally, Franco woulda jacked this punk by now. But. He knew where this kid came from. Knew he'd probably been through some fucked-up shit. *But why exactly was he givin Franco so much shit?* "Okay. Soon as you give me one good reason for turnin me down. And no more bullshit. Like a *real* reason."

Ray hopped down the steps. Still towered over the former world champ. "Cuz my sophomore year I fought your son!" Ray was right in the old man's grill. But had to hand it to him. Guy stood stalwart as Ray's unhitched home.

"You guys got bad blood?"

"Nah we squashed it. Run with a lot of the same kids when he's in town. But ya know. Complicated shit." Ray spared Franco the Lenore love triangle shit.

"If it's squashed... Then it's squashed."

"So what now?"

"Brawlers. Two o'clock. Every day."

AC. Finally. Five years since the day. Franco met Ray.

Ray popped in the locker room. A specimen who had elements of all who surrounded him. Joey's boulders for shoulders bulging his athletic T. Brazil's mile-long legs dwarfing his trunks. Taz's bony knees and bows all exposed. And Nelly's hands for grabs and throws.

All while Franco begged for mercy over Ray choosing "Mercy." Franco had suggested other songs by Kanye to Ray. "Power." "Stronger." Anything but the superficial "Mercy." But Ray showed no mercy.

Franco led the charge out of the tunnel...

Then had to throttle back. Into an awkward walk. His fighter had slowed down. Busy pointing. Nodding. Waving. As Kanye rapped about lambos n hos. Which made Franco wonder. Did Ray have that other part? That had set Franco apart. Drove him to perfect his art...

The home crowd thought so. Whooping it up for the local boy about to engage an enemy from overseas.

Ray peeled his t-shirt off. (Solid blue. The sponsors would be adding their imprints with a win.) Spread his arms for inspection. With the bod of a god...

Giving Franco faith. Hell, where was Franco at Ray's age? Full time at the docks. Side hustle for The Frog. *Semi-pro* fights in AC. Now here was Ray. Surrounded by a veteran team. Already fighting for The Show. And that's when the lights went low...

Over the speakers, a foreigner crooning. As the crowd was booing. In disapproval of the goon. Entering to "Mi Patmutyun."

31

Franco watched as Aram "The Arambie" Gesheva descended. With his hollow eye sockets. Fluid motion. A zombie. With the gait of a vampire.

And backed by The Beast. The man who took Franco's attention. The man with hair everywhere. Except his head. The man strapped with the strap. Umar "The Beast" Basayev. The champ of the 185-pound division for five years running. As if he'd had enough of beating on Franco and the boys down at 170.

As Franco and Basayev continued to trade looks...

Ray opened with a hook. His long, strong limbs suited him well as a striker. A striker who could deliver all four with force.

Aram was the inverse. Stout with twice the girth. A grappler first. So he laid low. A submarine waiting to submarine the battleship's plans...

The battleship that fired and fired. Missiles that mostly missed.

Others absorbed by Aram.

Ray was connecting at least...

So he finished the first round still firing with haste. All from his slender waist.

In the corner, Coach Franco told his surrogate son. "You won round one..."

Ray sucked wind as he rapid-tapped his foot.

"...but you gotta be patien—"

Ray was already popping away—

The ref signaled and he was popping away...

Dancing around Aram.

Firing and firing.

Until...

His tired arms went limp.

Until his dance... slowed to a limp.

That's when The Arambie mounted and mauled him. Like it was the first MMA fight ever. Invented on a beach in San Diego back in the day. When two teenagers, one a wrestler, one a boxer went up against each other. The grappler easily won. More of the same in UFC 1. The tournament taken by Royce Gracie. Tanglin up big guys like crazy.

While the game had changed a lot since then, there was still a certain DNA in MMA. And on that day, it was revealed to Ray. The results blindsiding the fighter new to The Show like he was a baby daddy on *The Maury Povich Show.*

Still, Ray writhed like when he was getting trashed outside his trailer...

Only this time, Franco wasn't allowed to intervene.

As Aram rear-naked choked Ray, revealing that ancient MMA DNA, Franco pondered some of his own. Some he wished he didn't own. A propensity to put all of his eggs in one basket. An MO he'd take to the casket. Back in the day, it was tunnel vision on his own career as his family life cratered. Then Ray gave him a second chance. And Franco was doin the same old dance...

He coulda been focused on building a business outta Brawlers. *And he thought he was.* It took a champ to build a camp. If Brawlers could make one outta Ray, they'd have clients all day. But now? Back to the bottom of the barrel. It'd be a couple years before they'd get another shot like this. In the meantime, too much rent to miss...

The Franco fight club now officially on its way out...

As Ray tapped out.

Franco scaled the cage. Watched the belted Basayev strut around like *he* had just won.

Franco then took a knee. Like Ray was T. "Ay kid. Don't worry about it. Gotta work on the ground game is all."

Ray rolled onto his belly. Hammer-smashed the canvas. "Fuck!" The only bluster he could muster.

As General Franco sighed. As fucked as Custer.

TRACK 5. WALL STREET WALLS

TJ HUSTLED ALONG THE WATERFRONT like Little Mac training for Tyson. Only this little mack didn't have a coach at his back. Dad was busy with another one. The surrogate son. Not that Franco could help T. His son in pain. His Cain. Franco was unable. Ray was the fighter. Ray was his Abel.

All TJ had at his back was a backpack. Although he had taken a page out of his father's playbook. Got after it every spare minute. Ever since setting foot on campus. Found a hole-in-the-wall resource room to get his work done without distraction. *Whether it's fightin or college or whatever, look at it like it's your job,* Franco had told him. And T did. Amazing what one can get done 10-4 Monday to Friday. Of course T also had to hoof it to classes before and after those hours, but all in all is wasn't bad. Till he added in the extracurriculars. Had to run Blue-Collar Scholars. Had to have fun at the frat house. Had to intern. All while the family business took a downturn.

As the ferry made its way to Manhattan, TJ made his way to its restroom.

He squeezed into the small stall. One with a toilet King Kong musta crapped in.

TJ hung his backpack on the hanger dangling by a bolt. Wishing he could bolt like he was Usain Bolt.

But the kid now in a sweater vest was too invested...

The kid who slipped as he slipped into khakis...

Dropped an elbow into King Kong's crap. *"Fuhhh..."* TJ let it drip as he ripped toilet paper. Then wiped it down the best he could. Pretended it was all good. At that. The Francos were good.

Office VPs to the left of him. Cubicle analysts to the right. TJ cuttin through the two. Hearing "Stuck in the Middle With You."

TJ banked a right into a pit of four cubicles reserved for summer interns. Only TJ's internship had gone into overtime. So he collapsed into his chair for the umpteenth time. In the cube to the back left. No one else left. The inhabitants from last summer sailing through senior year. Offers made and accepted by all three.

There was The Machine. He had sat in front of T. DiCaprio face. McConaughey hair. Sheen lifestyle. The legacy employee may have moved in Dad's shadow at the office, but he had launched his own legend on the New York City nightlife scene. The summer before. Would party till four. *On weekdays.* Then sober up on an elliptical before dashing to his desk for the morning bell. Say hi like he's all swell. Then drape his suit jacket on his chair. Put his monitor on anti-sleep. And head to the nurse's office. To count some sheep. He'd regroup and grub with the guys at lunch. Or as he called it, breakfast. Tell them all about the night before. The parts he remembered anyway. The knocking some bridge-and-tunnel asshole out. Then banging the guy's girl out. Wild. The cutting to the head of the after-party line at Pisa's. Then walking out with someone else's pizza. Sick. The passing out while a rando gave him head. Then waking up to wetting her bed. Epic.

In the other front cubicle was Supra. A wasian girl who'd split her childhood between private school and private lessons. The latter for athletics *and* academics. A ladder that led her right to Harvard and recruitment halls full of investment banks. Giving *her* the thanks. *We're desperate for a talented girl in our ranks!* Ha. She and her homegirls were crushing their coed counterparts on campuses across the country. And *in-style* for the buttoned-up girl who left her top buttons unbuttoned. The *hime* who told her prideful papa that her Supra nickname was in honor of those sports cars he loved. Ha. She'd have a helicopter. *And they called her cubemate The Machine.* Supra was the real machine. Getting it done at the office all day every day. *I'll get on that right away! All night I can stay!* While the others went and had fun. The inebriated entitled ones. Sure, Supra had privilege. But she also had the privilege of knowing the difference between that and entitlement. She was using her privilege to keep climbing higher. Rung by rung, stepping on the necks of asinine analysts more concerned about their fantasy football teams. All without paying any mind to her campus's latest game. The identity shame. She was *proud* of her claim. Her Anglo half had architected the country and her Asian half had shoveled shit in it. Without grovel as they laid gravel. Made sure their kids didn't unravel. Her grandmother had picked produce–yet produced *her.* By the end of last summer, the powers that be were *begging* Supra to sign at their place. She even figured that, among all of the analysts, she finished in first place. Of what she liked to call, the "super race." The phrase that sparked her nickname in the first place.

And there was TJ's back cube counterpart. His childhood friend and now fraternity brother, Lance. T had scooped the econ minor to the chance. They'd even walked into the assembly of final round interns together. But something about the tribunal was tribal. TJ and Lance joked that there was a wasian flock. And a blatino block. And as TJ tagged along with Lance to the latter, they'd also noticed that the gaggle of girls had made their own huddle altogether. At the end of the day, the powers that be must've drawn-and-quartered the cohort the same way. Cuz there ended up being an intern offer for half of each contingent. Same for when it came time for full time. Either an intern got an offer or didn't. Simply story. Save for the lone intern in purgatory...

Hey guy. You go to school nearby. How about college credit to continue your grunt work?

Sure, that'll work!

April and still working. TJ took a breath as he fired up his machine. Figured his spot went to The Machine. As for Lance, T was happy for him. He wasn't recruited against the underrepresented undergrad anyway. And no doubt Lance had his own obstacles. Like the scandal at his first college. So yeah, Lance deserved his sail through senior year. TJ just... wished he was sailing alongside his fraternity brother. Like they were Brennan and Dale in *Step Brothers*.

The monitor illuminated T's bloodshot eyes.

Still, T excelled on Excel. Every summer intern could use the program without a mouse. Keyboard commands were quicker. Made the higher-ups richer.

"Ay oh. TJ Francooo," began the disembodied head on the divide. The one topped with an overgrown mop. "How's the Camarooo?"

The hanging head a reminder of all that snow. Two

winters ago. The investment bank had only sent their back-office operation to T's campus. So T ran his own operation. He canvased. Spent winter break walking Wall Street. Handing out résumés. Cold-crawling. Up and down the Financial District. Up and down Midtown. Trudging through snow with ankles of ice as executives iced him out. But for every ten, one would take his résumé. Then keep him by the phone till May. But for every ten of those fakers, a real taker. One who would take the time to circle back. *Thanks but no thanks.* So easy with email.

When the snow settled, so did the final numbers. One thousand executives approached. One hundred who took a résumé. Ten who took the time to get back. One who asked him to interview.

A junior executive actually. The disembodied head currently haunting T. Mitch. An associate who had enough pull for the intern pool. But had so far lacked the lifesaver to bring T aboard full-time.

"I drive a Mustang." *But want a Kamara.* TJ smiled over the words that played in his head. *The date. At eight...*

Mitch's incoming arm launched a report onto T's desk. "Latest 10-Q for Synthol. Need to update the model." Mitch drove home his point with a two-finger point, "Bada bing bada boom?"

"Yeah like my full-time offer."

The disembodied head rose. "Brotato..." Then bobbed over to T's cube...

Mitch's red tie rested on his belly like his athletic laurels. The 26-year-old golf god with dad bod. "I'm *charging hard* for you. *Going to bat* tomorrow morning. Peters is in town. I am *running this up the flagpole.* I am *escalating* this motherfucker." Mitch's finger having fired in a different direction with every expression.

And T had turned his head up at the mention of Peters. Mitch's boss's boss. The managing director who could call the shot himself.

"He wants me to update him on this potential merger." Mitch tapped the new 10-Q on T's pile.

"I'm on it." TJ grabbed the financial filing.

"Email the mod this evening. We'll touch base Monday." Mitch fist-pounded T. Added sound effects as he blew it up...

TJ exhaled. Flipped through the 10-Q. Soaked in the numbers as others ran through his head. *Should have the model all updated by six. Showered and changed by seven. Date at eigh–*

"Oh. Pitch deck too of course," said the disembodied head once again haunting T's cube.

"I can't– I've got a date–"

"JWoww can wait."

T pressed two fists into his mouth.

"Brotato... It's a joke."

"So you don't need a new pitch deck?"

"JWoww was a joke. I def need a new deck." Mitch's head rose from the divide as he threw on his suit jacket. "And when you do get back to Jersey... You see Pauly D, you call me." Mitch held up a thumb-pinky phone. Then extended it to a *hang loose* on his way out...

As Mitch disappeared down one end of the hall, an old friend appeared at the other...

The demon. Waving from the door to the high-rise terrace. Enticing T to cut like Ferris... *Come on, forget all about this zoo. Lenore, Branchton, Brawlers too. And of course... you know who...*

Sick as my secret
Just wanna secrete it
Drag it out beat it

But it's undefeated

TJ rubbed his neck. Stress stirring up his past better than his late grandmother makin gravy...

So the kid with papers piled head-high. Popped a pill to get his head high.

Then threw on his fleece.

And got to work like a beast...

TJ's mind was in overdrive like Bradley Cooper in *Limitless*. The kid making sense of paperwork limitless. So out of his mind, he'd lost track of time. One had turned to two to three to four. As his spreadsheet tabs grew from two to three to four.

TJ closed it and opened the PowerPoint deck. A Boov toiling for Smek. *A fleeting reminder of a weekend home. Taking Kyd to see* Home...

TJ re-worked slides 55... 66... 77... As five turned to six turned to seven...

The trooper in his Cooper stupor reviewed the whole deck...

Emailed it to Mitch. And was out that bitch.

Headed straight to his date. At eight...

"GREEDY! CORRUPT! WE NEED A CHANGE ABRUPT!"

TJ tried to cut down the alley but it was too late–

Classmates from JSUH. The Wall Wall Streeters. Cutting off the alley with their signs and their chants. Leaving T no chance...

"GREEDY! CORRUPT! WE NEED A CHANGE

ABRUPT!"

Two cops had cut a path. That a protester lay in to obstruct pedestrians.

So T hopped over. Like it was fuckin equestrian.

"Sure just walk all over her like you walk all over everyone!"

"He's Wall Street!" convicted the Contemporary Culture classmate. *Sori.*

"One percent prick!" charged a puncher in a peace sign shirt– *Anders*–

TJ grabbed the puncher on instinct. Took him down like he was back on a high school wrestling mat. Only with a mob on his back.

TJ held onto Anders more for dear life than to extend the fight–

"You drive a Lexus!" lashed T.

"My parents didn't give me a choice!"

The mob toppled T as Anders piled on...

"I'll have to sell it when I'm unemployed! Thanks to you capitalist pigs!"

"It's not my fault you majored in–" T's retort was shortened by the splash of tar that came his way. A splash that also caught Anders–

And just as T was about to weather the incoming feathers...

The capitalist pig... was saved by the pigs.

TJ wiped his partly tar face. One cheek blemished like he was Scarface. So when he said he didn't wanna press charges, the black cop called him a saint. But TJ told him he ain't. It's just... he had a date. And he was gonna be there. *At eight.*

TRACK 6. KAMARA

KAMARA SAT AT THE OUTDOOR TABLE under the heat lamp. At the Italian restaurant that rested on a corner congested.

She watched Washington Ave. Hoboken's main drag. Checked her phone. Five minutes to eight. Why didn't she wait? *Stop, you could've lost the spot.* Still. Was she being rude? Was he an old-school dude? He'd picked this hole in the wall after all. Should she stand? Should she call?

Kamara bopped her forehead. Making much ado about a minor thing. Was it a minority thing? A female thing? Or. Just a human thing. And here she was going on and on. Why couldn't she... just be? Just hang like the tablecloth on the two-top. Which reminded her of her tube top. What if a boob popped? She went to put her flannel back on— Ugh red and white checkers. Might as well drape it on the bussed table next to her— *Just... hang.* Kamara took a breath. Yeah just hang. Like her hair. *Her hair.* Was it too frizzy? Too busy?

The thought spun Kamara's head back to her middle school days. When she first labeled having "black" days. Like she was Soundgarden. Dark as James Harden. After baking on the beach all summer. After the salt, the sea, the humidity... poofed her hair to the nth degree. Gave her an apple tree top to match her bottom. And damn how *that* blossomed. The boys sure thought it was awesome. Ass *and then some*. The teacher meanwhile... thought the black girl was dumb! Talked a little slower to her than the rest of the class. Like they were smarter than her ass. Like there weren't butthead white boys and in-space Asians. But nah it was *her* persuasion. That sparked a most unforgivable deed. *Teach asked if she could read!* From her brain she could bleed. Instead she would smile all sweet like a Swede. At least according to the stereotype. She bet the country had all types.

Then on went Kamara's seventh grade year. She signed up for cheer. And as the days lacked light. Her skin got light. The cool calmed her hair. And sick of the teasing, she started to tease it. The tree top now a flowing willow. She'd even dyed it yellow. Even that boy Dylan said hello! That was on her "white" days. Toward the end of the year. Classroom expectations shoved up everyone's rear. *And* she was captain of cheer. Team picture of them all hugging, so fond. She was just one of the blondes! Like she had started the year on some Beyoncé. Then somebody schlapped her into Kimberly Schlapman. Looked just like her mother. You'd never know. Her dad was a brother. Back then like she had two sides. Flipped to black or white like a chip in Othello. Like she was sometimes Desdemona. Sometimes Othello.

But she was over all that. Her teenage drama. Even the family trauma. She'd worked it all out in counseling. Knew who she was. But the date anticipation. Still gave her a buzz...

TJ approached from the waterfront. Still wiping his cheek with his removed fleece. He'd reduced it to streaks.

"Hi!" Kamara shot up. And as she extended a hand, better saw the young man... "What happened?"

"Wall Wall Street," TJ said, motioning back. Then realized he was still holding her hand. So soft in the weightlifter's callused claw... He let it go as they took their seats. Saw the shock in her cheeks...

"Are you serious? I'm supposed to go tomorrow." Kamara put her hands out. "To peacefully protest. Executive accountability."

"Peacefully? They could've used you."

"My dad always used to say. The crazies come out on full moons." Kamara nodded to the full moon over Manhattan.

"Howoo..." cooed T as he shifted to his un-tarred side.

As Kamara smiled.

As the waiter dropped off water. Asked for their order...

TJ motioned to Kamara's menu. "Did you get a chance..."

"A couple minutes please." Kamara's request served to the server.

TJ meanwhile folded his hands under his chin. Dove right in... "So I intern on Wall Street. How about you?"

"Well. I'm a psychobiology major..."

"Oh man that's too bad." TJ shook his head.

Kamara tilted hers. "What's wrong with being a psychobiology major?"

"I only date sane ones."

Kamara processed it as she sipped. Then laughed and spit—

Water all over T's face.

"Omg I'm so sorry!"

TJ wiped his face. "Nah it's fine. Help get the last of this tar off."

As well-adjusted as she was. There were still triggers. Her father and *his* dark half. Figuratively speaking. If only that could've been wiped away. Instead, half her childhood was wiped away. Sure, there was the good half. Her dad employed. Unannoyed. Playing toys. But the other half. Was no laugh. He'd belt her and belch. The segregation-era infant now fully grown. Teachin her what he known. When he was once again for hire. As drunk as Bunk from *The Wire.* Shoutin about how he'd beat her black off. Leave her better off. Like her white bitch mother. Who started fuckin another. When she'd had enough of the brother. As in black, Jack. As in her husband who blew it all on blackjack.[4] Once fed Kamara crackerjacks. For dinner. One minute a devilish grinner. The next a crying sinner. If only his hair was thinner. If only his pigment was winter. Then he'd get into the union his in-laws were in. Wearing their shiny jackets with their chapter numbers or whatever they're called. How could a nigger know? A nigger that knocked and no one showed. Standing there at the union hall doorstep. *How could no one answer,* he'd tried to mull it. Oh that's right, cuz he didn't have a fuckin mullet. Just a 1990s nigger knocking. And they called *running away* nigger knocking! As *they* hid inside the hall. Smokin their Pall Malls. Prolly still wearin those jackets. Those ones with the waistbands as tight as the stranglehold they had on all the good jobs. The jobs that allowed them to sit around and bullshit. As the black man was left in the mist. Brooding like Ice Cube. "Guerillas in tha Mist."

Lord what kinda life is this! Still Lord. I never used fists. It was just smacks. Just hits. And never in my baby girl's face. Lord I was wrong I was out of place. It was just... discipline. This world. I want her to win. And okay, yes, that one time with her mother I went too far. But I would never. With my dear Kamar. Baby girl, I hope you can hear me. Wherever you are. The best for you, always, I pray. With love. -Greg Day.

The girl at the Italian restaurant was having a minute.

---

[4] *Boy are brown people welcome in casinos. Come on, win some C-notes!*

Damn she could get lost in it. A well-adjusted 22 and could still get stuck on two. When Daddy would prop her on his chest and make her heart melt. The next day. The belt. Her bottom a welt. As her mother's brothers drank, smoked, and joked their way through life. While her father's was rife with strife. Whether he did wrong or right. And nah she wasn't trippin. She'd never approve the whippings. The ones passed down from generation to generation. The ones that traced back. To a slave nation. So yeah, Kamara could understand. Cries for reparations. Not that she needed any. She had done the preparation. But what if she had come from a worse situation? She could account for her mother being an accountant. Like how she could account for disconformity in the black community. Tweaking terms like *whippings* into *whoopins*. Just so they could own. Some language of they own. Or the term *cracker*. Kamara always thought it meant *white as a cracker*. So boy did the college class revelation attack her. The term meant *whipcracker*.

Kamara whiplashed to the present like she was Miles Teller. Now what did this boy's eyes tell her? She'd watched his mood vacillate all semester. Even online-stalked the rap jester. But his look in class... something festered...

"Ready?" asked TJ.

Kamara darted her eyes back to the menu. The one she'd been holding for the last few minutes...

The returned waiter waiting...

"I'll... have a burger," concluded Kamara.

"Een Eetaly. We have meatball."

"Oh. Yeah. Meatballs. That's what I meant."

"What kind?"

"Cloudy with a chance?" burst the flustered girl.

TJ burst with laughter. Then after a sorry to their server–
"Wanna split both kinds?"

"Perf."

As the waiter whisked away–

TJ and Kamara laughed away...

"Cloudy with a chance!" cried T.

"Tell me that don't sound good!"

As the laughs settled, the smiles remained...

"Quincy Jones song by the way." Kamara pointed to the surround sound speaker crackling above.

"Sinatra," retorted T.

"Obvi. But Quincy produced it. He and Sinatra were like this." Kamara crossed two fingers.

"Is that right?"

"That's damn right!" shot Kamara as she shot upward.

A tense moment. Until–

"Okay then!" laughed T.

"I don't even know why I said it like that!" laughed Kamara. "By the way, you want Italian?" Kamara motioned to the restaurant at-large. "High school choir. I sang in the Sistine Chapel."

"I'd ask if that's right," began T. "But I'm sure it's *damn* right!"

TJ and Kamara shared more laughs. More smiles.

Under a full moon. As Sinatra crooned. That Quincy tune. "Fly Me To The Moon."

After dinner, as the two marched on Washington, TJ stayed to Kamara's left. It put his stained side aside. Not to mention it elevated him on the tilted sidewalk. Turned his few-inch height advantage into four. Over the girl five-four. *Just like Lenore.* Nah... this girl was more. T wasn't even tryin to score. Except in their argument. As they strolled on cobblestone. Snacked on Cold Stone...

"How could you say Kendrick is better? Two albums. Eminem has eight!"

Kamara nibbled on Neapolitan from her mini cup. "I prefer quality over quantity."

"Still. You can't be telling me that Kendrick is already a better rapper than Eminem."

"I didn't say a better rapper. I just said... *Better.*"

"What does that mean!"

"A better person."

"Oh you know them now?"

"If you don't think they're in their art..."

"We're judging artists by the kindness of their content now?" TJ tossed his large cup of cookie dough.

"I'm just saying... I like what Kendrick is saying. Kendrick... is my dude."

"You *like* what he's saying? What's your favorite song of all-time? The fuckin song from *Barney*?" slurred T. He'd only had one drink. Oh and that pill.

"You can't mess with lyrics like *skid-a-marink-a-dink-a-dink.*"

TJ stole glances at the golden girl. The cheer in her full cheeks. Her smile of perfect teeth. Her smooth face without a wrinkle. As she threw in a wrinkle...

"Ooh this is my turn." Kamara motioned down the crossroad. "I'm meeting some friends at Maxine's. You're welcome..."

Ha. No T wasn't. He'd been there already. The music club featuring every music alternative considered "alternative." Emo rock. Experimental EDM. Mumble rap. The crowd as eclectic. Hipsters. Punks. Lo-fi tough guys. All united in dyed hair and piercings. Tats and tattered clothes.

"I've got plans," began T. "I can walk you though." T stopped in his tracks. *That recent class lesson...* "Or is that like...

chauvinistic?"

Kamara crooked her head. "Demanding would be chauvinist. Asking? That's... chivalrous."

TJ flared out his elbow out. Made an accompanying creaking sound. *"Errrttt."*

"Armor's a little rusty. Gonna have to shine you up," concluded Kamara as she latched on.

As the two strolled down the lane, TJ's mind strolled memory lane. His rap act was a big hit at frat parties. The DOG house bangers that packed the mansion's first floor. TJ pacing across the homemade stage. The campus's very own Lil Wayne. Bringin the pain. Pacing, crawling, crouching. Pants slouching. As the party ball spun the hall into a kaleidoscope of colors. Illuminated coeds bouncing in hystery. At the best parties in history.[5] TJ breathing fire as his childhood homeboy Dragon blazed a beat from the booth. The DJ & TJ.

Dragon bakin the beats...

TJ cookin the hooks...

> *"Rock the mic like Rocky*
> *Clock the flow like Franco*
> *Jersey to Frisco*
> *Place jumpin like disco"*

TJ didn't think it his best work. But Miley. Had taught em to twerk.

Then at Maxine's. It flat-out didn't work. The open mic. Run by that dude Mike. Who rode a unicycle bike. TJ thought he was gonna crush it. Following the rapper with purple dreads and a tatted head. Stumbling and mumbling on-stage...

---

[5] Agreed upon by the DOG brothers in a unanimous vote.

"Sumpinsumpinsumpin
Government!
Up to sumpinsumpinsumpin
Corporations!
Up to sumpinsumpinsumpin
Dealer!
Gimme sumpinsumpinsumpin"

TJ had to cover his ears over the minimal beat and maximum noise. Man was it *sumpinsumpinsumpin.* But it had everyone... *jumpin?*

Then TJ's rap. They couldn't give a crap. In fact. They thought it was whack.

TJ snapped back. To the present scene. *God damn* her beauty beamed. So he left out the fail at Maxine's. Stashed it next to The Thing. The fucking Thing. Perfect evening. But once again creeping. Crawling. Into his consciousness. Up until then, it had been a minute since they'd talked. A nice forever as they walked.

TJ's hands in his pockets. He'd thought about putting his arm around her. But another recent class lesson. *Microaggressions...*

Kamara saw the crease in his face. And why did he pick up the pace? There was something about the guy... The boy really. Twenty-one goin on 12 if you asked her. With his baby face and big browns. And his little hair poof. Pointed forward like the bow of a boat. Flimsy doe. Like it could be blown any way the wind took him. Like in class. Lost in daydreams. Or. Were they nightmares? His face turning to dread. *Something* weighed on his head. Something she couldn't figure out from all her internet stalking. That began after Dr. Goa had assigned them to be peer review partners.

Their papers on cultural representations in athletics. Code to talk about systemic injustice. NFL plantation structure. Gender pay gap in professional sports. Kamara herself focused on instances of inferior women's facilities. An A after TJ's peer edits. Boy contributed like a subreddit on reddit. He both built on her argument *and* went off on tangents. Like how he gave her the tidbit about the US Women's National Soccer Team. Having to play on turf while the guys got grass. An insult to the world-class. Followed by notes that made her laugh. *Make sure to mention Carli Lloyd. Straight outta Jersey. Best women's player ever! Some people say I look like her btw. Maybe I should wear a wig for Halloween. Tell everyone I'm dressed up as a g— good soccer player. I sucked as a kid! Not like my sister, Kyd. She plays tennis too!* Crazy boy boy boy. And *his* paper... boy boy boy. He went a whole other way. Had something *positive* to say. Kamara could remember the first page...

"Little Man. Big Game: How Lack of Accommodation led to Innovation." This 2015 NBA season, three hundred-odd athletes are playing a game. Then there's the artist. Reinventing the sport. His canvas the court. The one too short. Too slight. Too light. Among 300 Goliaths, a kid. Succeeding the same way David did. By slinging the rock. His quick-release shot. From unimaginable spots. His dribble on lock. Weaving. Leaving opponents in knots...

Page after page, Kamara's face had stayed buried. And ever since, she'd been following Steph Curry. *And really? A B? Even after her edits? Starting with adding subtext to his subtitle. Switched it to 'When Weakness Causes Strength.' Still, guess his paper didn't have that one strength. That one hers had. A message that didn't mess with Dr. Goa's ideas.* Of course Kamara couldn't say any of that out loud. Instead, she started stalking the irreverent rapper on AudioCloud. The things he'd say out loud! Maybe... *she could get up there one day...* No way. *They'd laugh her away...*

And the boy's rhymes were clean. The boy now walkin

her to where she was a queen. Right then the two in-between. The DOG house and Maxine's...

Kamara hugged herself as they hoofed it. "Chilly all of the sudden."

TJ put an arm around her all of the sudden. Got all worked up all of the sudden. Until her soft shoulder warmed his cold hand. Calmed the young man...

The young man who went to bed that night recalling the moment from another angle altogether. From behind...

Him on the left. Her on the right. In the moonlight.

Arm-in-arm as they walked. On the uneven sidewalk.

Yet as they passed a budding birch. Passed an old church.

The two stayed attached at the hip. How beautiful that night. How steady their ship.

TRACK 7. SCREWED

NELLY OFFERED RAY A HAND.

But Ray popped himself from his belly.

So it was Franco. Who took it from Nelly.

And by the time the ref raised the winner's hand...

Ray was in the stands. Hopped out of the cage as the rest of the fight team was hopping in. Joey. Brazil. Taz. Wearing their old team T's. As faded as their futures as their future star faded into the tunnel.

The commentator with the crew cut and cut muscles carried on. Benny "The Force" Forsado. "Aram, I have to ask. How do you feel about your opponent running off?"

Aram responded in his native tongue...

Basayev, belt slung over his shoulder, stepped in. *"He say, real fighters don't quit so easy."* While Basayev's words disseminated to the fans, his eyes locked on one man. *"He say, real fighters not afraid to lose."* Basayev shrugged off the boobirds. Added a point of his finger. *"And he say, real fighters do not run off."*

Franco watched as The Force forced the issue. The issue of The Show trying to goad Franco into a superfight. Launch into the now-sanctioned New York City right. Franco the local legend with a vengeance. The American's last loss at the fists of Basayev, The Beast from the East. "Umar Basayev. I can't help but notice that, as you say these things, you're looking and pointing at Franco."

The crowd erupted at the mere mention of Franco.

As he and Nelly shared looks. The two in the cage feeling the heat. Like it was old times. Only now. They were old guys. Franco's hair grazed with gray like a black Cadillac sideswiped. Nelly's buzz cut meanwhile receded like a North Pole iceberg.

"Listen to this crowd!" crowed The Force.

"Americans so easy to lionize one of their own," barked Basayev. *"I. Beat. Franco."*

As the crowd beat back, "STERRROIDS... STERRROIDS..."

"Excuses. Like their 'champion.' Torn ankle. Same as me. But I come back. Bigger and better. Beat everyone. Still. Everyone want to talk about Franco."

"Everyone talks about me?" Franco inquired to Joey at his other side.

"Maybe not in your suburban soccer mom land. But in certain circles of the Internet... Especially after his Tweet..."

Basayev bellowed louder. "One title fight! *One!* The Show give him a shot against The Prince. Then he give *no one* a shot! Run away retired!"

Scattered boos...

Brazil patted Franco's back from behind. "Forget this guy."

"Yeah. Who would want to remember that beating anyway?" tacked on Taz. His joke going over as well as Franco playing dolls with Kyd.

Brazil slapped Taz in the shoulder. *"Come on, man..."*

"Jeez. Everyone so sensitive in their old age."

The Force swooped over. "What say you, Franco? A lot of people had *you* as the winner in your brawl with Basayev..."

The crowd roared.

Franco shrugged. "The match's decision was final."

"RE...MATCH! RE...MATCH!" chanted the crowd.

The Force smiled with delight under the lights. "Like Basayev Tweeted. Randy Couture was a champ at 46. How old are you?"

"Just turned 41," sighed Franco.

"You're a spring chicken!"

"RE...MATCH! RE...MATCH!"

Franco leaned into the mic. "My decision to retire was also final."

Franco made for the open fencing.

And as he and the team were bailing...

Basayev continued the railing... *Test me any time. Anywhere. And I still beat Franco again. Any time! Anywhere!"*

Franco and Nelly slammed the doors of the Charger. Franco reached across–grabbed glasses from the glove box. "Night driving."

"You consider that Lasik?"

"Kind of expensive no?"

"Healthcare..."

"We bought the bare minimum through Brawlers. And it's still a backbreaker." Franco reversed the Dodge out the spot. "School plan's probably pretty good huh? Get me a job as a gym teacher?"

Nelly exhaled a small laugh. Its size matching the amount Franco was joking.

"Or maybe AD. You're just about out huh?"

"Twenty-five in and five to go. Looking at a house on the bay in Brick."

The driver took a breath. Too bad Nelly wasn't looking for a house in the burbs. Franco knew of one in Branchton he'd like to get rid of. One he bought at the height of the market in '08. And now owed just as much on in '15. Oh wait, actually owed *more* on. Took out a second mortgage like a moron.

"TJ couldn't make it tonight?"

"Yeah no. Busy with school. Interning."

The Charger crawled along the downward spiral of the nine-story garage. Like Dante descending the nine circles of Hell. Each question from Nelly burning Franco further...

"T like the gig?"

Franco kept on a car's ass. Considered a pass– "Yeah I dunno. Work is work. Pay is good though."

"How is he otherwise?"

Franco turned up the AC. *Couldn't wait to get the fuck out of AC...*

But the only pedal he was pushing was the brake. A few more questions and he'd break. "Seems good. Been playin tennis with Kyd Friday mornings."

The further Franco downward spiraled, the redder the sea of taillights got.

"You see him much?"

"Between Brawlers... Kyd... Julie... Ray..."

"Hoboken's beautiful," nudged Nelly.

"Birthplace of baseball n Sinatra," concurred Franco.

Nelly glanced at Franco's arm on the wheel. Usually it was his left. Tonight, his right. The shielding shoulder filling out the team T in full. Triceps stretching it further yet. Veins flooding his forearm. "That arm. Basayev should've thanked you for retiring."

"His is even bigger." Franco rolled his window down for fresh air. Like a crashing plane passenger to a mask.

"Lot of dead weight he put on after they upped the testing."

"Winning regardless."

"Weak division."

"One eighty-five though. Big boys."

"Slow boys."

"Too bad there ain't a senior division." Franco rolled down the rear windows. Which only mounted the pressure from Nelly's still being up. Guy just wouldn't give up...

"You wouldn't qualify. Not enough miles on your tires."

Twenty fights. Fifteen and five. Franco's final record. Only one of those with the added tax of championship rounds. All in all he had about half the cage time of– *the guy currently rushing across the red-lit lot–*

Basayev. On foot. Charging with his crew. Toward a familiar dude–

Ray. And his homies. Fronted by a dude as scrawny as his clothes were baggy. His bark as loud as he was little. Screws. Franco knew the punk from that time he came into Brawlers. For a day on a guest pass with Ray. Till Franco caught him sniffin yay. As Screws must've been again that day. Based on the dumb shit Franco heard him say–

"Ya'll niggas ain't shit! This ain't no cage. This a street figh–" Kid was finished before his sentence. The punch sent his chin sideways, his knees buckling. Ray's flock already down a duckling...

Maybe Nelly was right about not enough miles on Franco's tires. Cuz right then, he was feeling as fresh to death as Ronnie Magro. On some, *Come at me bro...*

Nelly though... was dialing on his phone. 9-1-1. As he watched Franco run... toward his surrogate son. His surrogate... *punk*. Man did Nelly hate sayin it. All the rough kids from The Wood he'd seen turn good. But if Nelly was being honest? He always smelled a skunk. Sure, back in high school Ray could dunk. But when he didn't have the ball? His shoulders slunk. For every three he sunk. Five he'd clunk. Then say his team stunk. As he walked tall in the halls like a hunk. And earlier that night... walking off like a punk. If it was Nelly's army? He wouldn't give him a bunk.

Ray who, once again, got tangled up by Aram. And dropped like a bomb–

Franco shot in to help–

Got blindsided by a Basayev boot.

Franco seeing stars as Basayev tossed him between cars–

The champ feasting on the main course. As his pro camp beat street kids with no remorse. The rest of Franco's fight team already headed home in separate ways. Not like the old days.

As ole Franco mixed it up once again. Circled as he considered some ground and pound. But Basayev's defense was world renowned. Maybe Franco should stick and move. Wait for the boys in blue. *Shit,* thought Franco. *That's when you know a street fight's gone bad. When you want the cops to come!*

As Franco froze with indecision...

Nelly had a vision...

Basayev's other crew. *His* homeboys. From *his* homeland. A land more hardscrabble than an Q-word in Scrabble.

Packed in their Rover–

Its tires spinning over–

The vehicle speeding over–

Headlights closing on Franco–

As Nelly rammed him–

And took the KO.

TRACK 8. G-SUS

G CLOSED HIS LAPTOP. In his editor's office on the hilltop. Time to close shop. His latest column for his campus's "conservative" publication complete. The label assigned over and over by Sori's rival outlet. The label that pained G as he tried to explain his columns were common sense. Like he was Thomas Paine trying to explain *Common Sense*. G'd call out the supremacists. The fundamentalists. The conspiracy theorists. But they either weren't on the campus or kept to their corners. Meanwhile. The culture crusaders paraded! The campus raided! Someone had to stop the thieves. So it would be the editor-in-chief. The double major acing English and History. Early admitted to law school–*Ivy League*. That's why G could gamble. Piss off the culture crusaders in class. But those whiney dopes. They were making plans. Buying ropes. To take down the statue G approached...

William the Third. Aka Old Willy. The original endower of the campus. Before the state claimed the estate. King's College turned Jersey State University at Hoboken. JSUH. Aka "J-Sue." Used to be "J-Suh" but "suh" was a term slaves used to answer their masters. What! Call G crazy but *he* thought "suh" meant State University at Hoboken! And what really fired G up was that the change supporters (or were they *sue*pporters!) said it was also insensitive to assume that SUH would be pronounced "suh" rather than "sue." Hello, the school had English roots! And this from a half-Jew! It all made G madder than Ndamukong Suh. He wondered if he could sue. But he had no ACLU. Guys like him could be offended too!

As G stalked the state U, he was reminded of younger days. When his mind first began to haze. When he'd first felt rage...

Walking home from fifth grade. Wondering if Mom was with her secret John. Little Gary had eavesdropped from the john. *Don't worry we'll be home free! Gary doesn't get home at three. I put him in aftercare. He spends two hours there.*

Mom and her picture-perfect house. Boy did it stand out! Their white house. That looked like the White House! Even had one of those black birds above the door. Better yet, it had a third floor! Hitched with pitched gables and dormer windows. Inside, an attic that was once little Gary's rec room. Until Mom wrecked the room. Turned it into an office slash workout room slash checkout room. Where she'd "unwind" with wine. Ha. Getting fucking trashed. As she yelled for Little Gary to take out the trash.

Yeah. Gary remembers.

School (and aftercare!) over and walking back. Thumbs under his backpack straps. Arms meanwhile crossed as he crossed the streets. What he'd learn later was a defensive position. *As he headed toward his home. Where the world was to leave you alone!* But Little Gary would slow... as he cut through the park... hoping the guy's truck wasn't parked... You know, *To do renovations.* Perfect. Another home wrecker.

Gary remembers.

Wandering aimlessly around the house. Bouncing a ball to himself. Waiting for Dad to come home. He'd track where his dad should be starting at 6:00 pm. It was Dad's hard-out time to leave the office. But as he'd explain to Little Gary, it was 6:15 by the time he'd actually gathered his things, made it to the elevator bank, waited, entered, exited, legged out the leviathan lobby and actually got out to the damn ave that was Amsterdam Ave.

Gary Senior would then bounce over to Broadway. Double-time it to Columbus Circle. A circle jerk of automobiles, buses, bikes, businesspeople, bums, bodegas, buildings. The New World's end-all be-all. Columbus looking down on it all. Others looking up. Calling for his fall.

As Gary's dad passed Sbarro and Subway. Herded into the subway. But not before he craned his neck for a fleeting look at Carnegie Hall. In another life, the working-class kid from Parlin... was the next George Carlin. But long ago, Gary Senior had turned the mic in. When he'd met Susan. She told the aspiring comedian to get a real job. He'd never beat the odds.

Little Gary and his ball would be banished to the backyard by the time Senior was barreling through the bowels of the city. *The bowels. Mom and her laugh-filled lessons. Of calling the subway system small intestines. NJ Transit the large intestines. Dad's train exiting the city like excrement. As Mom laughed, 'Hee-hee! Maybe I should do comedy!'*

As Senior scrambled around Penn Station like one of those rats he saw back on the tracks. Trying to be a hero to his boy by catching the final express. Like he was Hero Boy catching the Polar Express. In that movie he had taken little Gary to go see. Mom saying, *Go without me. I have plans at three.*

The old 6:59 express. Unless. There was a delay somewhere. A protest at Columbus Circle. Or the hundred-

year-old subway encountering one of its hundred problems.
Or the NJ Transit train running late. Or getting delayed. Or
having a breakdown of its own. Not to mention a traffic jam
leaving the downtown lot. Little Gary would go through
every scenario. And what if Dad had to take the 7:16 local?
So many stops, it was loco. The little foreign language learner
begging to stay up, *Just un poco.*

Just lay in your bed then! she would yell from her den.

So Little Gary would rest his head on his glove. Clutch
his baseball. And drift to sleep. Dreaming. Of a wolf and a
sheep.

G now all grown. Still walking alone. At least he had an
ally in Old Willy. G shared a point and a nod with his old pal.
His old pal under threat of attack by the dopes and their
ropes. Forget that the man literally endowed the grounds they
all walked on. He married his 15-year-old cousin! *Uh maybe
because that's what people did back then... No G, because he was evil!*
Deemed so by unaccomplished crusaders who'd been
pampered since zero. They were the heroes! They were the
righteous! And by ~~God~~ (wait, something other than God
because you can't say God) Old Willy was gonna get his due!
Well. It'll be G they'll have to go through.

G carried on through the campus pavilion. Past outrage
booths that numbered a million.[6] So inclusive, so plural! In
their exclusion of the Christian, the rugged, the rural. Look at
them acting so pious. Ha. They're loaded with bias! Like that
booth manned– excuse G– womanned by Sori. M.O.M.
Move Over Men. So righteous! Not divisive at all!

G continued past Sori's man pyre. His head on fire...

*Just because an acronym works doesn't mean you should use it!
Most moms would disapprove it! And move over who exactly? My dad?*

---

[6] Rough estimate by G.

On his train broken down in Glen Ridge? Ohhh the privilege! And wow Sori, you must really hate... Bill Gates! The guy who has the guts to drop out of Harvard. The drive to change hard drives. Endure the eight hundred ulcers and million migraines that is being a self-made success. And what's his capstone creation? The Bill & MELINDA Gates Foundation! So is he a tyrannical, patriarchal one percent white man? Or is he... the fucking man! Appreciated by his wife and vice versa. And why do marriages keep infecting G's head like MRSA!

G would've loved to say all that. But he kept it under his hat. He'd had enough of being shut down for this and that. So he would just save his at bat. For the bigger game. Throw Sori's whole mob out at the plate. Because Willy, too, would have safe space.

Did Sori see him walk by? OF COURSE she saw him walk by! How could you miss the guy? As if he wasn't tall enough. His mop popping higher yet. As his long legs strolled without a care in the world! Thinks he owns the world!

Same as the day Sori met him. Back when they were freshmen. A hook-up more depressing than "The Freshmen." Heck, after that, Sori *welcomed* settling for a nerd. But they were all infected. The entire herd! Oh how it drove her face to scorn. Boys openly talking about porn!

Sori recently checked it out herself, not that she wanted. But she'd heard about this upcoming doc, *Hot Girls Wanted*. And what she saw, she's still haunted! Little windows of bigger boobs. Lips. Hips. And not just valley girls turned vixens with voluptuous extensions. Young women worldwide! Caked in perfect makeup. With ethnicities, eye colors you couldn't make up! Pop-up videos of every shade from brown to yellow. *Blowing kisses to Sori, saying hello!* Naked girls in the shape of hourglasses! So impossible, Sori put on glasses! One day she was even late for classes! Gone down an endless hole of endless holes. *Gaping. "Mock" raping.* Yet it was *Sori* with the choke in her throat. When a girl took a footlong down her throat! And there wasn't one whore... there were four! And each of the tricks... had magic tricks! One with her ankles past her ears as she started to squirt! Another doing a manic twerk. As if she had gone berserk! And the other doing—*wait, how did that work?* And wouldn't that cause an infection—ATM?? And all to see for free—who needs an ATM!! Not men! They don't need anything but a keyboard and cream. As they keyword and cream. Who needs a real girl when you've got a machine! *Ooh she could just imagine G all manspread. Watching some dork get head. Then giving a line of wagging waxed asses smacks. As the bimbos' fake lashes batted back!*

And not just G... Boys everywhere! Pleasuring themselves like they *deserve* the bombshells and their shaved labia. Like they're princes of Saudi Arabia! Women out of this world for everyone to see! Every Tom, Dick, and Harry! No wonder the campus boys with their subpar parts and beer guts... were cheersing and calling girls sluts. Pig faces acting like they should be dealt four aces. *Want girls to act like pornstars? Then act like action stars! I'll facial. I'll ATM. I'll threesome. Soon as you start jumping out of cars and planes and then some! It's all fake for goodness sake! Vaginers gushing like geysers! Girls moaning with cheer as they get stuffed in the rear! Such insatiable MILFs, stepdaughters, and PAWGs! UGGHH MEN ARE SUCH FUCKING DOGS! Oh and one last thing, G. With your skinny ass and big head. You're not THAT fucking handsome! So stop acting like you're owed a king's fucking ransom!*

"*Ugghh!*" was the only part Sori said out loud.

But as she stared that statue down...

Her frown turned upside down.

Because Sori couldn't wait.

To take Old Willy down...

G continued past the ridiculousness. More outlandish than *Ridiculousness*. Reminded him of that grade on his paper. He grabbed it from his satchel. Read the brilliant title back to himself: *Talkin' Bout My Jenneration: An examination of shifting cultural values that propelled both a gold medalist and a reality star to fame*. Followed by... that big, fat F.

If G knew in high school what he knew now... he would've locked himself in his room until he aced Calculus BC. Like he was Pythagoras in 500 BC. Then he could've gotten a full ride to BC. Christ, where they're still allowed to say *Before Christ!* But like Mom's taste, the school was too expensive. Instead G's at state U and on the defensive. Everything about him inherently offensive!

Such bad guys! G, Old Willy, and the names etched. Into the library he passed next. PLATO. VOLTAIRE. KANT. *They couldn't exist now, they kant! Reason is out. Rights are in! Can you talk? Depends on your skin! And forget achieving. We all win!* The culture crusaders should scrub those names out fast. Before people remember the *other* past. The one that wasn't aghast. The one of free thinking. Accomplishment. Now it's all about entitlement. Indignation. In the Me-Me-Me Nation. *Ask not what your country can do for you, but what you can do for your country.* Holy crap! The Lodin clan's favorite Democrat said that! And when the latest Lodin recalled the first Republican president, he even started blinkin. The answer... was Lincoln! American politics. What a trip!

And G's walk. What a trip!

The confused kid finally unwound on the winding walkway. The walkway that led to a magical land still standing. While the outrage tornado had wound through the rest of campus, G's Oz still stood. The final stronghold. The mansion a hundred years old. The campus pillar with white pillars. Its grand banner billowing in the wind. A most welcome sign no doubt: THE DOG HOUSE.

Delta Omega Gamma. Of all the fraternities, this one was Bama. The perennial number one. And "G-Sus" was their number one. The Hudson River air flowed through el pres's hair. Yeah G-Sus walked. Hearing "Jesus Walks." Kanye doin his thing. Saying we're at war. *With everything.*

Light and wind burst as G pulled open the mammoth doors.

He continued into the expansive hall with soaring oak walls. The living room sight such a beauty... Four brothers playing *Call of Duty.* Bye-bye campus ass backwards. Hello hats backwards. Fingers firing away. As they all said hey...

"G-Mannn..." huffed Baby. The five-ten 200-pound... *Baby.* Because of that one time he played Justin Bieber's "Baby."

"G-Unit!" deep-voiced Dexter. His real name was Lester, but he was obsessed with *Dexter.*

"G-Sus!" same-timed Mummy (the half-Brit always calling his mummy) and Khalid turned Krypto. Famous for playing things close to his bomb vest. Some joked in jest. In the space. Safe from arrest. Where being offended. Was given a rest.

G gave his men a salute and carried on. Past bongs and beer pong. The place clean, the pledges gone. G had them over earlier that day to get everything in order. And *damn,* even the plants were watered. Like when freshman G was taking the orders.

The ascended president ascended the grand stairs. His footsteps echoed off the soaring ceilings. In the palace. That could absorb his feelings.

G passed four brothers crowded around another big screen–high-fiving and screaming. Playing the downstairs crew and apparently smoking the fools. They didn't even notice their dude! *Hey it's me, G!* But they were locked on the screen...

T's boy LaCroix. (Or as T calls him... Lance.) Famous for mid-party shifts to the flavored club soda. A nighttime practice the helped him make morning lax practice. But right then firing away along with Moe, Larry, and Curly. Named so by G when he caught the three stooges... watching *The Three Stooges.*

"Currrlyyy," called G...

"Garrryyy," returned the kid who everyone else called Candyman. The health nut would never have a piece, but he dated a girl named Candi.

G carried on into the last room on the right.

Saw T curled up on the pleather couch to the right. Curtains drawn to black out the light.

"What's the matter with you?"

"Nothing. Napping." TJ's demon belly laughed from behind the curtains. *Nothing! Good one T!*

"Fuck you. Something's the matter." *Fucking T! We've got it all in our suite!* Posters of hoes. A bookcase of bros and their prose. Our very own bar. *We're BMOCs. We're stars!* And speaking of stars. TJ's old desktop Dell. The one the fool was going to sell! Until G had the genius to load it with the inappropriate. So their laps would still work appropriate.[7] G the PC pimp. Their whole set-up so pimp! Yet...

TJ's curled up on their couch in the dark. Listening to...

---

[7] G would be remiss to not give credit to "Hudson from Ithaca, NY" for sharing the idea on a Bill Simmons Grantland mailbag.

Linkin Park?

"I didn't get the job," droned the outcast wolf of Wall Street lying under a poster–*The Wolf of Wall Street*. Mitch had told T not even by phone–just a text! *Sorry no go good luck with what's next.* Eight extra months in the bullpen alone. For those eight final words on his phone. And what *really* ran TJ's face as red as a tomato? *Mitch didn't even take the time to call him brotato!* But. That was an hour ago. Now? The kid's face was as flushed as his future.

The demon laughed his ass off again. *Huh-huh-huh. Right. That's your problem. Huh-huh-huh...*

What exactly was so fucking funny? wondered T. Then closed his eyes over the whole thing. And saw... The Thing. That even more haunted highlight reel. The one where the demon. Was real.

Ah but G-Sus saves. An hour later, he had T slamming shots. The Fireball putting out the fire. T and his half-Jewish homeboy now so far gone. Listening to *So Far Gone*. A Lil Wayne n Drake. Listening to Wayne n Drake.

"I'm Goin In" assaulted the surround sound. Bass popping as Wayne popped off. In T's one-minute tally, Wayne called his friend a motherfucker, pissed and shit on said friend's toilet bowl, let Crystal suck his pistol, blew her brains out, then killed his friend in the kitchen...

As T rapped along so hard, he was twitchin!

G & T! Drinkin G & T's! From their red Solos. Shoutin Yolos! *To think, just an hour ago, T was staring into the abyss. But now this!* And he had G to thank. An interview at his dad's bank!

T bobbed his head to the beat. Feelin it. Gettin lit. Remembered he was *VP of the DOG house. Had the biggest room in the house... Yeah he and the Pres had come a long way...*

Since meeting that freshman day...

One from working-class Woodbridge. (T had left out the part about his Branchton years.) One from wealthy Wayne. One with one parent on-hand. (Dad had to coach a fight. *No big deal, it was aight.)* The other with two. One short. One tall. One lacking. One with it all. At least T could leave his dark years behind once and for all...

The freshman roommates shook on the fresh start–

TJ.

Gary.

TJ watched as both of Gary's parents adored their boy. Reminded TJ of *his* good old family days. *Before Ray.*

The three parents left the two boys alone. One was used to it. Gary told TJ he had done summer camps and study abroad. TJ replied that he had also studied abroad. *Her name was Lenore.* G picked up on the joke that was the first of many...

G & T. Gifted & Talented by day. Gin & Tonic by night. Two knights. Ready to conquer the world.

But the world fought back. T's first panic attack. He thought The Thing could be left in Branchton. Until he crossed paths with an old classmate in microeconomics. Sitting next to him, causing a macro problem...

Aren't you the one who...

Maybe it was a lot of things leading up to it. Too much partying. Too much pizza. Not enough sleep. Not enough–T couldn't really name it–*warmth?...* as he lay in his cold dorm. And all the pressure. To get A's. To get laid. To look good. No only in real life but online too. Facebook Instagram Snapchat Twitter. Scrolling your phone while you're on the shitter. TJ was already on edge, he could do the math. But it was definitely that crossed path. That sparked his dark past.

The one he thought was vanishing. Until it caught him at the edge of Jersey.

A demon that slithered into that econ classroom, grabbed him by the throat—cut his breath. Wrung his palms with sweat. *And shit... was T about to shit?* Be publicly embarrassed all over again? And what did the professor just ask? *Can you say that again? No, I'm not talking to my friend! He asked... to borrow a pen!* T furious with both men! The prof and the pupil. Darting between both with dilated pupils. Kid losing his scruples. Like an Indian-Russian looking for ruples—

So panicked, he could flip his desk over—

He didn't. But a month into college. It was all over. The dream. Of living the dream. Like those kids Little T would see on Saturday afternoons. When he was done with cartoons. Those kids living the best years of their lives. Yelling *Roll Tide! R! U!* And *Go Blue!*

While College T was just... blue.

I said, aren't you the one who...

Nah dude. Who are you?

Deny deny deny. Bury bury bury. Prolific as Tyler Perry.

Meanwhile the demon kept growing. *TJ terrified—where is this all going?* Like when he sat on the cramped campus bus. Worrying he'd go nuts! *What if what if what if...* this and that and this! The repeating thought endless! But he kept it all in. Till he was so sacked, he couldn't get off the rack. He'd lay in his bed all night and see terrible sights. *The attacker. Charging like a linebacker—*

The first dashes of dawn proof of a new day. Proof of survival to TJ. He'd get an hour-and-a-half of sleep. One solid cycle before dragging his ass to classes slow as molasses. But still. He made it to every lecture. Noted every conjecture. Like that professor saying they were just matter. So... *did life even matter?*

After a month of sleepless nights full of terrible sights, the psychology cynic checked himself into the health clinic. And one month into JSUH. They told him he had PTSD.

T did the occasional therapy. A revolving door of grad students. Catching up on his history, then soon after history. At least the prescription was rock steady. Some kinda pills called Clonium. And damn did they clone him man. Had the kid thinking clear. Released all his fear. Had him pretty good for a couple of years. But lately, the senior wasn't seeing so clear...

Mm but the Clonium and those drinks so clear...

Those G & T's. The ones G & T were drinking right then. On that senior Saturday afternoon. As Wayne & Drake rapped that sick tune.

As T built up enough liquid courage to ask of some news...

"By the way, when I walked in earlier. The downstairs Duties[8] were saying something about defending Old Willy..."

G lasered in on T. Narrowed his eyes... *Those fucking guys...* "You're not gonna tell Sori's roommate..."

"I've hung out with her once..." T left out the part about their upcoming date as he sipped from his Solo.

"The crusaders are planning on taking him down. The day of professional school graduations. When the cops are distracted all over campus. Between your business school, engineering, pharmacy, etcet..."

The biz major had to impale his relieved exhale. "So, what are you gonna do..."

G pulled his old aluminum bat from below the bar. The one he kept on-hand in case of any altercations. Rival

---

[8] The house's *Call of Duty* addicts. Who, in group texts, are also referred to as "Doodies."

fraternities cranked on drugs. Sports team thugs. State U kids from the wrong side of the tracks–weekends waving in their whole pack.[9] Oh and who could forget the local vatos locos. Crazier than spring break in Acapulco. "It's only fair that someone protects the campus from vandals." G held his bat high with two hands. Ready to play his own... *Game of Thrones*.

TJ paused his pour from the gin handle. "You're not seriously going to hit a girl..."

"Of course not." G admired the ball marks on the barrel of his varsity bat. "But will I defend myself again a sorry ass yes man? When he pulls a Mace can? Hell fucking yes, man." G took some practice cuts.

"Are you nuts?"

"Are *you* nuts? They're the vandals!" G pointed his bat to the campus at-large. "They don't get violent, I won't either. But if I have to defend myself on my way back from some ball with the boys..." G leaned on his bat like Poppins on an umbrella. "No big deal. Nothing of your concern. Just knock out that interview, will you?"

"Yeah. Okay." What else could T say? Yeah G was bein slyer than Stallone. But he was only gonna go *First Blood* if *they* drew first blood. And it's not like T owed Sori any favors. So why the fuck would he be a savior? Gettin involved was fuckin absurd. And the Clonium concurred. The lines no longer blurred. For *rell*. Like T was Pharrell. G looking like Robin Thicke. His hair just as thick. Walkin around with his stick...

The scene had T so out of his mind, he ran "Blurred Lines."

As G danced over. Did a line.

T passed. Said he was fine.

---

[9] Not T and his boys. They were cool.

Then two-hand poured another gin & tonic...
One hard. One sweet.
Not that he could tell which one was which.
Once they were mixed.

TRACK 9. FULL NELSON

CARS FILLED THE LOT. THE LAWN. THE LANE. Law enforcement wasn't enforcing. Rather escorting. An endless line of incoming cars into neighborhood driveways. Owners making them loaners. For the sad occasion. The final ovation.

The church burst at the seams. Every pew overpacked by a few. Other attendees spiraled up the spire. Overlooking the altar altered. The square now loaded with chairs.

Franco saw these people for days as he stood at the dais. His conscience as stained as the stained glass. The towering slats depicting struggles of mothers. Of brothers. Their tint hinting at light beyond. But letting little in.

Everyone there gathered for the man of the hour. The man to Franco's right. He could barely stand the sight. The man he'd looked to so often. Now in a Costco coffin. *How could Franco stand and deliver? Someone give him some Jack, let him ruin his liver.*

Franco looked beyond the casket showered with flowers. To the barrages of collages. Of Thomas "Full" Nelson the Ninth. First grade and standing on a first place podium. High school yearbook photos. One in a wrestling stance. One king of the dance. His Rutgers University cap and gown. (Or Rutgers, *The State University of New Jersey*, as Nelly would note to out-of-staters when they were on the road for Franco's fights.) His National Guard photo. The actual beret on display. Part of two whole walls devoted to friends, family, and fellow faithful. Then another wall. Boasting every team he ever coached. And every class he ever taught. He'd joke at the end of every season, at the end of every school year, *I want proof that I survived you knuckleheads.* Then would add, *And vice versa.* A hundred teams between those at the high school and those of his own kids. Including one golf team when the high school needed an emergency sub. Nelly holding six a.m. practices and his six-month-old son. Eighteen years of his history classes. From 1989-2007 AD. Before they made him AD. *A few thousand* kids impacted by him, Franco figured.

Before the service, Franco had looked over it all. Including the final wall. Dedicated to the fight team. The fivesome making fists outside Franco's Mustang. Suitcases tied to the roof. So young, *Oof.* Photos of Franco and Nelly getting matwork in. (The Nelson family graciously omitting any of Nelly nailing Franco to the floor.) Then that one photo. The action shot post-Franco's championship fight. Joey and Brazil helping Franco out of the cage. As Nelly held the belt high. Toward the—*no, for the*—Woodbridge faithful on-hand.

And the Woodbridge faithful were on-hand once again. Bigger by a factor of ten.[10] Having traveled from all over. Still in shock that it was all over. *Franco wanted to shake Nelly awake. Let him know it was all a mistake. It was Franco's life they wanted to take. Those thugs gone on a private jet. Evading arrest. Franco about to*

---

[10] Or was it a "multiple"? Franco made a note to ask T later. Shit, Kyd would know soon enough.

snap–

Then snapping out of it at the sight of Kyd. Sitting there with her pony-tailed hair. No idea her father was *this close* to insane. *This close* to living back on Bunns Lane. The former champ now a one-hit wonder. His soul needing an asylum from becoming Soul Asylum. And, hell, that comparison was nice. When the Eminem fan realized. *He was Vanilla Ice.*

Franco looked to where he'd looked so many times before. Next to Kyd–to Julie. Her all black deepening her blues. Deepening Franco's moody blues. Like the Francos were The Moody Blues. But where was the fourth member? Where was T? Franco looked out at the sea. Saw the kid in the corner out the corner of his eye. On a first step up the steeple to get a view over the people. Musta been running late. School. Or work. It was always one or the other. Probably still looked like a cute enough kid. For anyone who didn't know him so well. But Franco saw the face swell... The eyes that fell... But Franco. His own issues to quell. So he remembered words from Coach Nel. *Answer the bell...*

"I worry sometimes."

Franco's opening words hushed the church. Like it was a concert and he was Church. Only Franco had taken his aviators off. Coach Nelson would have his ass if he kept his sunglasses on inside. They were tucked into his suit. All black everything. Like he was Jay-Z. In the same suit he wore 16 years before. For his old man's funeral. Only difference now was Franco had a black tie tacked on. Thanks to Nelly teaching him how to tie one in advance of Taz's wedding...

Your old man never taught you how to tie a tie?

He taught me how to tie one on.

Belly laughs back on that day. Back in the day.

"I worry a lotta the time. All the time these past few days." Franco glanced from stained glass to glass. To the pics of his teacher from history class. "Until today."

Franco straightened up. "We lost Nelly. Mr. Nelson. Coach Nelson. Couldn't be a bigger loss."

Heads sunk as the words sunk in.

"But. The gains already in."

Heads rose as Franco's optimism rose.

Franco soaked in the tear-soaked faces. "I see doctors, lawyers, nurses, teachers. Bankers, plumbers, coaches, preachers. Role model moms. First-class fathers. Turned-around teens. All back to see their coach. Their teacher. Their church leader." Franco took a breath. Took in the crowd's breadth. "The one we've all looked to. On how to conduct ourselves. In this fight called Life."

The heads stayed high as the tears flowed.

Franco wiped one away. "Ever ask him how he's doing?"

The mourners laughed.

"Coach how you doin?"

They finished for Franco–

"How are YOU doing? That's how I'm doing!"

Laughs. Outlasted by tears.

"Then there's his family."

Franco looked to Nelly's family. His wife, Grace, sitting up with grace. Her collarbones cutting the colored pattern atop her black dress. As she watched her husband rest. Watched Franco's address...

"He'd be the first to tell you. His wife is stronger than him."

Grace put two hands to her chest.

Franco nodded, looked to her left...

"Then you might worry about his kids."

Tommy the Tenth, a first-year teacher and coach, wore the town colors. Black suit and tie. Red shirt. Same colors Dad was wearing that day. The middle one Marina wore her marine wear. ROTC at TCNJ. Then their youngest, Zachary. The Doll Face Destroyer. The wrestling champ headed to Dad's alma mater for some Big Ten tilts.

"Until you remember. They're *Nelly's* kids."

Hoots. A–

"Whadaya say now, WOOD!"

"I say... we're gonna be okay," wrapped Franco.

He motioned to the choir...

Three elevated rows. In alternating robes. Red and black. Faces from white to black. As varied as the ages of the singers. From current students to some of Nelly's first.

The sight could make Franco burst. Spill his organs as his old classmate played the organ. *Francis Freeman.* The market genius retired. *A free man.* Making Franco suddenly surmise... *He'd be imprisoned till the day he died.* A faithless man who would never be free. Guilt. Obligations. Debt. That was Franco's G.O.D.

Franco walked over to pall bearer. As morbid as Paul Bearer. He took a last look at Coach as the choir sang...

"Your only Son
No sin to hide
The Lamb of God
Your gift of love they crucified"

Franco put a last hand on the man's heart. As if it could infuse Franco. *Man did the situation confuse Franco. He damn near coveted that basket. He'd switch places– Nelly just ask it!*

But the reverend dashed it. Closed the casket.

Franco lifted the front. As the choir sung of an affront...

"The humble King
They named a fraud"

81

Franco was joined by Tommy the Tenth, Zachary, and the last three... Nelly had dozens of to choose from, didn't he...

Days before, Nelly was laid up in a hospital bed. Bleeding in his head. Drifting in-and-out of consciousness. Asking forgiveness. For that time he said the wrong thing. Did the wrong thing. Ninety-nine percent of the time, a good man. But it was the one percent that weighed on his head.

That and a pall bearer decision.

It was then on his hospital bed, a shade from dead, Nelly took his wife's hand. And delivered the plan. Told her the fight team best represented him.

To which Grace replied, *Along with the other pall bearers of course.*

To which Nelly replied, *Along with you and our daughter of course.*

To which Grace replied with an eternal smile.

As Nelly walked off. On the green mile...

Nelly's two sons. And the chosen ones. Franco. Brazil. Joey. Taz. Six pall bearers doing the unbearable.

Amazing what ya could surmise in a passing look. Someone's face a one-second book. That's all it took for Julie's big blues. To ask Franco what he would choose. *Fight? Or lose?* Then TJ's drowned browns. Reminding Franco of pain beyond the immediate. But how could Franco mediate? Then Ray. His brownish-grays. Was he willing to fight another day? For shit pay? Or would he bail on MMA? Smoke purp and get cray. In his eyes. The options weighed.

The pall bearers rest the coffin atop rafters.

Hours later, Franco still there. As frozen as Elsa in *Frozen*.

The CAT-driving gravedigger finished maneuvering like Gravedigger. Then left him alone. The Pooh missing Tigger.

As yet another animal hopped over. The Frog. Fifty feet from where he last met Franco. When the two ex-mafiosos exchanged heated points at gunpoint. Then went their separate ways.

And now back in black like they were AC/DC.

The elder Frog gone gaunt. His helmet of hair in-tune with the tombstone...

Gray. Polished that day.

Thomas Nelson the Ninth. Husband. Father. Teacher. Coach.

"I would've made sure it said 'Athletic Director,'" croaked The Frog. One of his gray wisps unwound by the wind. As he took the last line in: *1968-2015.* "Goes quick."

Franco was sunglassed eye-to-sunglassed eye with the once mighty man. The gangster Franco once parted. To be trained by the departed. But here Franco was again between both men. Like the fork in his Road of Life led to the same place after all.

"You picked the right horse," concluded The Frog.

"We had some good years," Franco said of the two men still standing.

The Frog waved off the sentiment. "Glad you're doin okay."

Franco likewise shrugged it off.

Two boxers dodging compliments they didn't deserve.

"How's Marie?" redirected Franco.

"Marie's Marie. Good. How's your son?"

"Good." Franco choked on the one-syllable word like it was an eight-ounce filet.

The Frog took his shades off. Franco's answer a shade off. "Tough thing, what happened to him. I wouldn't know what to do."

"Yeah I dunno. He's smarter than me."

"Smarts and wisdom are two different things."

The Frog's hazels were dead even with the orphan's.

The orphan busy looking down. At the stone figure. His father figure. A title formerly owned by The Frog. The guy... Franco couldn't look in the eye...

The Frog reapplied his shades. Gave a final nod to the grave. "He had both in spades."

The daylight started to shade. Behind the church Nelly's ancestors made. The one The Frog had once flipped off. But that part of him was switched off. Thanks to the man in front of him. Still standing. Like he was at the end of his last fight. "The horse you chose? Keep riding it."

The Frog once again unfurled his middle finger. Along with an index. Kissed them and touched Thomas Nelson the Ninth's tomb. Then walked off. Picked up a path into the forest...

Left Franco all alone like Forrest. Without a Lieutenant Dan. Left to craft his own plan.

Could Franco fight once again?

Could he be a man?

TRACK 10. THE GIRL & THE WOLF

THE BLACK MUSTANG CRUISED past them tough little Turnpike towns.

TJ patted his chest twice as it passed Exit 11.

"For Woodbridge right?" asked the passenger to his right. Her goldens like two lights. On the rainy NJ day. "You lived there before Branchton."

"Internet stalking much?"

"You don't catch up on people when you start following them?" Kamara left out the internet stalking that preceded recent follows and friendships.

The driver shrugged as the car powered through a thunder shower.

Then trucked past Rutgers...

"R.U. Rah Rah!" hooted Kamara.

"Scarlet Knights fan?"

"My dad used to take me games there. Back in the Schiano days."

"The good old days," sung the 21-year-old pilot like he was Twenty Øne Piløts. "When Ray Rice was a good guy."

Kamara took a breath. *Ray Rice.* Beautiful wife. Beautiful

life. Until he went crazy. Down in AC. Lost it all in the blink of an eye. *Why did it bother her so much, why?* Because she knew the story. In all its glory. At least Ray Rice was making amends. To the cause a friend. And what if he... had CTE? And his dad. Killed in a drive by. How did that affect the guy? And didn't Kamara's dad not have a dad either? And didn't he–the D-3 DB–grow up tackling head first? Complain his headaches were the worst. Did anyone care? These are things Kamara didn't share. No she didn't dare. Her roommate would give her the chair.

Don't get Kamara wrong. The fools deserved what they got. Treatin their wives worse than thots. But when? How big an amends? For a second shot. And could she ever... give one to her pops?

TJ meanwhile was in his own rut as they passed Rutgers. He loved head coach Schiano. Once an assistant to... Paterno. On the same staff as... Sandusky. *It all made T's head so fuckin dusty.* On some *sick* degrees of Kevin Bacon. Fryin his head like bacon.

As the kids' minds wandered, the Mustang wandered into the woods of Jersey...

"In my glove box, can you hand me the magnet?" T motioned to his AC vent. "Hang up the nav."

Kamara opened the glove box. Grabbed the obstructing composition book. One of those classics splattered black-and-white. The owner's name written on the center label: GEMINI.

As Kamara handed over the magnet, as the driver set-up his phone, she gave him a look of her own. Muscles and a jawline. "Hot" in the teen soap opera sense. But a bit of a nose. Could use a few inches. On some Ryan from *The OC.* "White." But second thumb on the iPhone white. From backstreets. But worked on Wall Street. Could be so charming. But his tortured look–so alarming. Focused on

GPA. But also T & A. Pics of him and his roommate with sisters at sorority mixers. And she'd caught him checking *her* out. Many times no doubt. The kid who was sympathetic to some causes in class. Others, he'd roll his eyes and pass. A sweet kid. But a street kid. Online pics with his sis–a cute lil gal. Others of unsavory pals. From Woodbridge. Or as some joked online, Hoodbridge. So yeah she understood why. He chose *Gemini*.

"You can read it. It's just rhymes."

Kamara opened to page one. Read it with a deep voice out the side of her mouth...

"Ya'll actin like ya Langston Huuughes
His problems was huuuge
The 1920s duuude
Would trade places witchyouuu"

TJ watched... Her full lips *smiling* as her goldens carried on...

"Then again he eschewwwed
Today's world so cruuuel
Slip with one false mooove
Forever on YouTuuube"

Ha that's dope!" concluded Kamara.

"Kendrick is your duuude. Well mine is Langston Huuughes."

"The black man from Harlem a hundred years ago?"

"Black. White. High-class. Low-class. Big figure. Small stature. Sometimes sloggin it in The City. Sometimes jet-settin all over the world. Sexually confused. But always..." TJ glanced the nav as he searched for the right word...

"...human."

Kamara's goldens met his gaze.

She then turned to the next page–

"Who needs heaven
When you're a heathen–"

TJ grabbed the notebook– *recalling a Kamara hook– If you don't think they're in their art–*

"Excuse you."

"Sorry. We're here." TJ stuffed the notebook away.

The Mustang moseyed through wrought iron gates.

Onto an expansive estate.

A sign on a stake:

WELCOME TO WOLF WOODS.

"This puts my dinner and ice cream to shame."

"We'll see," said Kamara.

"Oh shit– One's loose!" TJ grabbed for Kamara, ran for his life–

Only Kamara had stayed put–

As a wolf charged on its hoofs!

The wolf leaped–

And licked her.

Kamara pet the dark guy as they stood eye-to-eye.

She then took a knee. Laughed at T. "What are you doing?"

TJ put his palms out. "I thought it was a wolf!"

"It is a wolf. Come here."

TJ eased over. "Looks like a... German shepherd?"

"Where do you think they come from?"

"Germany?"

"From wolves. They've just... been domesticated over generations."

TJ went for a pet–

"Not these guys, though. They're direct descendants of wild wolves."

TJ yanked his hand back.

"Relax. They've learned a new way here."

TJ looked out at the meadow. Where a pack of wolves ran. Looking like Siberian huskies and German shepherds. Only... *meaner?* Their bodies leaner. Their muscles stronger. Their snouts longer. Teeth sharper. The size of the incisors...

"This is Tyson. Scar pattern around his eye," Kamara indicated with a roll of her index. "Got attacked by a bear when he was a pup. Fought him off, then grew up prone to fighting. Wasn't allowed near people."

"What happened?"

Kamara nuzzled the unmuzzled beast...

"Love."

The wide-eyed kid mulled her answer. Mulled the wolves in the meadow. "You come here a lot?"

"Senior thesis is a lot of work. I'm titling it, 'Nature vs. Nurture. Biology vs. Psychology.'"

TJ scrunched his brow. "What about... 'Nature is Bio. Nurture is Psycho.'"

"That's what I meant," declared Kamara as she noticed–

Tyson lay on his back before T–

"He's submitting to you. Pet him..."

T reached with the hand of a kid who never had a pet growing up. Only recently had Franco and Julie gotten a puppy. For Kyd.

As TJ successfully petted the submitted wolf, he looked out to the running ones. "So if I go out to that field... those wolves won't eat me?"

"I don't know. You look pretty delicious," quipped Kamara with a tap of T's cheek.

"Then you definitely better not go out there," returned T with a poke.

"It's all about how you treat them..."

TJ let the Frisbee rip.

The wolves ran. In just a clearing surrounded by trees, it seemed. But for T... a field of dreams. Standing there on the golden grass with the golden girl. The day's gray cut with pink rays...

As a wolf leapt ten feet high. Pulled the Frisbee out of the sky.

TJ threw his hands up wide. "Did you see that!"

"Yes," Kamara lied. She was busy watching his lit-up eyes.

TJ in turn looked at the girl. Hair dancing in front of her face. He wanted to take her–dance all over the place. The girl shearin his heart like Sheeran. But T didn't say what he was thinking out loud. As his head played "Thinking Out Loud." He simply wrapped his hands around her waist. Kissed her as they stood in place.

Kissed her as the wolves raced.

As the wolves jumped–

And licked his face.

"Back to Life" played in the Stang as it returned the kids to the edge of Jersey. The night as dark as T's car. City light drowning out stars. When he was asked by Kamar...

"Do you want to come over?"

TJ almost fell over. Like he was Super Grover. Kyd's

favorite character. T's bewilderment out of character. *Always dtf. So wtf. All actin like she's a bae. You've hung out twice ysk. T! Omg! Stop makin such a bfd. LFG!*

TJ followed Kamara into the brownstone that looked like something outta *Girls*. The living room even boasted a poster of *Girls*. Another one of P!nk above the pink couch. The other couch lilac and stacked with pillows. In-between, a glass coffee table used for anything but coffee. Incense, JUUL pens, women's mags. The tiny table on a knockoff shag. Which was on yet another carpet. Candles everywhere...

TJ sunk into the lilac couch. A nice reprieve from pleather. And the pillows... Fluffy and feathered...

A roommate thundered down the stairs... A thin redhead with a hoodie over her head. Making for the front door...

"Whoa, slow your roll, girl–"

The girl turned her hooded head. "Oh. Hey. Just on my way to that movie–"

"We can go with..."

"That's okay, Candi's coming."

Candi with her hair pulled back, hoodie pulled down, made her way down...

"Candy girrrl," sung T.

"Gem!"

"You two know each other?" inquired Kamara.

"You're not the only one dating a DOG," ball-busted the blonde hugging it out with T.

"We only play 'Sugar, Sugar' for her every party."

"Right after 'Baby'," laughed Candi.

"Well, that leaves you two," concluded Kamara. "Ruth, TJ. TJ, Ruth."

"Nice to meet you." TJ reached out a hand...

Ruth pulled a hand from her hoodie, met it.

"Ruth's an events coordinator. I told her about you–

excuse me–*Gemini.*"

"Oh cool. Yeah, let's stay in touch."

"Yeah. K." Ruth nodded and made for the door.

"Off to The Hunting Ground! Probably not as fun as it sounds..." quipped Candi on their way out.

"They don't strike me as hunters..."

"It's a movie about campus sexual assault."

"Oh. Yeah def not as fun as it sounds..." agreed T. "Worth watching though?"

"I mean it's not without its criticism, but some of the stories, general awareness... def worth seeing."

"Ruth seemed... eager..."

Kamara took a seat on the couch. "Want the long story or short story?"

TJ plopped back down next to her. Cozied back into that couch. "I've got all night..."

"Two weekends ago," began Kamara as she took a breath. "She hooked up with this guy at O'Brien's. And he was like, '*Wait till I get you on my home court.*' And Ruth was like yeah okay, whatever. They were drinking. Dancing. She forgets a comment like that even happens. Then last weekend. First time at his place. Soon as she walks in, he slams the door. Manhandles her onto a bean bag. Smothers her. He's like this big guy– She's yelling– *What are you doing– Get off–* Into his upper body crushing her. She had on a spring dress, so it was like wam bam–as she's trying to push on him– as useless as that was. You know, for the whole minute it lasted."

"Holy shit." T's jaw remained dropped.

"Then he puts an arm around her. Says, 'Welcome to the Darrell Dome.' Asks if she wants a drink! And she gets up. She's like, *You're an asshole. That was effed up.* And he's like, *Don't you remember? We talked about this...* She's like so flustered, she bolts over to our honors dean. Tells her. Then she calls the police."

"And..." *The fucking Thing... The ensuing investigation...*

"We'll see. It's a whole process now."

The college kids took a breath. Held it like they were holding for the outcome.

Kamara lit candles around the room.

As TJ was cozied into the couch further yet. "You know, lights work much better..."

"But candles are good hygge."

"What's *hoo-guh?*"

"It's means setting a nice vibe. It's Danish."

"Whoa, big-time cultural appropriation alert."

"Stop," laughed Kamara as she smacked TJ on the shoulder. "Besides I'm half-white. Maybe my mom's *from* Denmark. Maybe she *made* these candles."

"All Danish women make candles now? I didn't know you were such a bigot!"

Kamara upped the laughs and lashings. "Do I need to school you on prejudice plus power?"

"Nah it's all good candle lady. Save me the waxing."

"Boy..." Kamara straddled him.

TJ went with it. Pulled her in.

Eye to eye. Warm body to warm body.

When they heard somebody...

At the front door.

Kamara's *other* roommate...

Sori. Dragging a canvas bag like she was a Hoboken hobo. She gave an eye roll to the two rolling on the couch. "I'll be in my room." But she got stuck. The bag too hard to drag...

"I can help," said T to his surprise. *To show that he was*

reasonable? Whatever the reason, he wasn't able–
    "No thanks."
    After Sori lugged the bag up each and every stair...
    TJ gave Kamara a wide-eyed stare...
    "Okay then."
    "I admit. She can be a bit much sometimes."
    TJ took a breath. Exhaled...
    "Roommates."

When TJ later approached the bathroom...
    He passed Sori's bedroom...
    Saw her sitting on the floor amid the bag's contents strewn about. *For the statue thing G knew about?*
    T tried to get a better look.
    Took a subtle pace–
    Sori slammed the door.
    In the snooping boy's face.

TRACK 11. SQUARE ONE

FRANCO STEPPED INTO BRAZIL'S DOJO. Buzzing like
Permian at the height of MOJO. As Brazil hustled like Flo Jo.
Overseeing hip throws. Correcting back rolls.

Brazil then demonstrated a roll of his own. On the red
mats that ran flush to the padded black walls. The academy
colors matching the master's belt.

Franco watching the black man in the black gi. Forty-
seven and had created his own little heaven...

The one who nodded for Franco to follow. Through the
claustro rear corridor. Past the academy trophy case...

Into an office with plenty of space...

Brazil sat on a stability ball behind his desk.

Franco sat on one on the other side.

"You still got it." Brazil put his arms out to signal
balance.

"I also got a fight with Basayev."

"Really?"

Franco wasn't sure what Brazil meant by that. Really as
in, *That's awesome!* Or really as in, *You're crazy, old man...*

Brazil's next comment was an indicator of which way—

"Up at 185?"

Franco nodded.

Brazil looked the five-niner from twelve to six. "What are you walkin around at right now?"

"One eighty-five," Franco said with a twitch of his head. A subconscious reaction to leaving out how he was 185 with clothes on. Sneaks on. Phone, wallet, and keys too. He was really more like 182.

"Basayev's walkin around 210," countered Brazil with crossed arms.

"Ain't that why the Gracies invented Brazilian Jiu-Jitsu? So the little guy could beat the big guy."

"But the big guy knows it too."

Franco absorbed the stiff counterpoint like it was a Basayev jab. Then got popped by the power hand–

"The big guy who's eight years younger." Brazil uncrossed his arms. "And by the way, BJJ's roots, don't be sleepin on Maeda, França, and Fadda."

"See? This is why I need you. For that next level."

"Same commitment as I had with Ray?" said Brazil as he looked past Franco– to an instructor waving from the mats–

Brazil stood up– Another six-three tree–

That got stumped by the stump before him–

"Head coach. Nelly's gig."

Brazil motioned to his instructor, *Two minutes.* Sat back down. Tilted his head. Same way he used to tilt it against the rear window of Franco's Mustang. The hum of that glass against his bald dome. As he gazed at plains, dreamed of home. All across the USA with MMA. As Franco drove with Nelly right behind him. And Franco's right-hand man to his right. Joey. Sitting shotgun as Brazil's knees needled his seat. (Taz meanwhile sitting bitch and needling everybody with insults.) Brazil always figured Nelly and Joey to be the top two. But here was Franco comin through...

"What about Joey?"

"What about you? Look at this place." Franco motioned to the bustling gym.

"Exactly. Got a lot goin on."

Franco thought MMA had blown up back in '08. Ha. Chump change relative to 2015. And this fight? *New York City. The Garden.* The rematch. The bad blood. The *really bad* fuckin blood. Enough coin to cover everyone right this go-around. "Name your price..."

Brazil gave Franco another twelve-to-six look over...

Twelve o'clock: Receded hairline.

Eleven o'clock: Crows' feet.

Ten o'clock: Signs of jowls.

Nine o'clock: Signs of... life. Franco's pecs impeccable.

Eight o'clock: His abs still rock.

Seven o'clock: Quads and knees cutting his jeans.

Six o'clock: Oh yeah. Franco and that ankle...

"How is it? Can it make a camp?"

"Made all of Ray's camps," began Franco. "All the advancements in surgery. Rehab. Nutrition. Thing has less of a hitch than before my last fight."

Brazil nodded as he mulled it all over. "And you been on some LeBron. Resting up for the bigger game."

"Exact..."

Brazil's exasperated instructor leaned on the office door. Black belt dangling from his white gi. "I'm sorry but Herc said he paid for a private with you."

Franco and Brazil looked down the corridor...

To Herc in his singular red gi. "Let's fuckin go!" barked the muscle mass through his training mask. The bane a real-life Bane.

Franco and Brazil shared looks over the local joker...

"I'm guessin you're in now."

"Oh I'm in."

Franco stood up. "Okay cool. Cuz it's not like one of your best friends is askin you to lead train the biggest match in MMA history or nothin."

"It's all hype beforehand. Let's see what the word is *after.*"

"Let's get to work then."

Brazil reached out his oversized hand like it was a claw from one of them Seaside grabber games. Only this one had a sure grip as it clenched Franco's mitt. Pulled him in for a hug.

Followed by a finger to Franco's chest. "Five-thirty every morning."

"What? Snoop and Dre ain't even done partyin by then..."

"Man, it's 2015. We gotta get you on some T-Pain. On some '5 O'Clock.' If that's even early enough from Branchton..."

T-Pain. T. Pain. Over and over in Frank's brain...

BEEP. BEEP. BEEP. *Dafuck? It was still dark out.* Oh right. The clock read in all red: *4:30.*

Franco slipped a bare arm out of his blanket. Checked the time on his phone. Same.

"Shut it off already!" whisper-yelled Julie. From somewhere beneath her down comforter. Down there with Kyd. *"And learn how to use your phone alarm already!"*

Used to be Franco that snuggled up with Julie under a single blanket. But their master bedroom in Branchton was their first that was big enough to accommodate a king. Accommodate their own blankets. Especially important after the thermostat stand-off. Franco kept dropping it to 65. He'd studied sleep for the fight game. People slept better when it was cold. Period.

Julie kept upping it to 70. People slept better when they were warm and cozy. Period.

They settled on 68. Fuckin thing didn't have a 67.5 and fuckin Julie with her fuckin math argued that 67.5 rounds *up* to 68. Then on top of all that, she tried to dump a fuckin down comforter on them. Fulla feathers that kept geese warm in winter! *Outdoor* winter! Fuckin geese had Franco's situation all sullied. Like he was Sully. Till one night he grabbed their old blanket. Kept it gully. Meanwhile Julie's wrapped up in down. Wearin a skully. Franco & Julie. Fuckin Mulder & Scully!

Franco also knew that darkness–pitch darkness–was key to sleep. But nooo, gotta leave the bedroom door open and hall light on so Kyd could come in. Middle of every night, thundering down the hall. Bare feet on bare wood. First time it happened, Franco popped out of bed, almost kicked the midget intruder in the head. Even after that, it took Franco a week to forget he was livin on Bunns Lane. To drop the instinct to attack. Instead, he had to listen Kyd do her business in the middle of every night. In the bathroom right on his right. Full of moonlight! Franco lying there as disgruntled as Tom Hanks in *A League of Their Own*. As Kyd peed like she was Tom Hanks in *A League of Their Own*.

And after all that. She'd stand at the edge of the bed. Backlit. Moonlit. With her arms out. Like a possessed toddler! A possessed toddler that smiled...

Until Dad smiled back. Kissed her as he lifted her to the reserved little pillow in the middle of the bed. Occasionally attempting to wrap her up in *his* comforter. But Dad was *too smelly and scratchy*. Mama was *soft and smooth*...

The crew usually got up together at 7:00. Franco on top of getting Kyd off to school. Julie off to Brawlers for open.

But now. This fuckin 4:30 alarm...

Franco cut it.

Dragged his boxer brief-wearing ass outta bed. *Four-thirty and had to get to The Wood.* And he's walkin around with morning wood. Like he was Steve Carell in *The 40-Year-Old Virgin.* Only he was *The 40-Year-Old Fuckin Idiot* who thought it would be a good idea to fight the number one fighter in the world. Wait, check that. Franco was so dumb, he forgot he was *41.*

Franco flushed the toilet, watched the water drain. Like his '08 fortune n fame. A reminder of why he was back in the game. But... *The fight game was supposed to be about more than money...* thought the ex-dockworker trying to think clearer as he stared in the bathroom mirror...

Franco sat in traffic on 287. The overnight construction crew still at it. The one that was set up *ostensibly to avoid traffic.* Instead, creating it as the construction run funneled from four lanes to one.

Franco's Dodge squeezed in place. In the nation's most stressed-out state. As some new song called "Stressed Out" played. The singer introducing himself as *Blurryface.* The singer that reminded Franco of T. When he made a wordplay with latter and ladder. *Yeah that's why the singer reminded Franco of T. Not because of the singer's... anxiety.*

Franco who, for all his years, was still an orphan who fought his way through 1980s Bunns Lane. A place where talkin about feelings was insane. But what about that counseling the foster kid did? Pff. Once a month group chats. Sometimes didn't even get the chance to chat. Learned more from the posters on the wall. Like that needs pyramid. The one the fighter started building for himself.

But how do ya help... someone else?

And T was all set with that Clonium, wasn't he? From the college pharmacy. And if the Franco health plan didn't cover any kinda psychology, how important could it all be? Less than a dentist cleanin your teeth.

Franco sucked all the air in the Charger. As he sat there. In a tail of taillights. Scanning the horizon for daylight...

Franco parked behind Brazil's. *Six-thirty*. Brazil's Suburban of course there. *Even Brazil was right there–*

Hocking keys at Franco's head–

"You owe me an hour. Round up my kids."

Franco caught the keys like he was Geena Davis in *A League of Their Own*. And why the fuck was that movie on his mind so much? And how the fuck was *he* Geena Davis while *Kyd* was Tom Hanks? By the time Franco was ready to give Brazil a rebuttal about how he only had six weeks–

The dojo door slammed behind the master's behind.

Franco climbed into the black Suburban. Settled into the leather seat. Started her up. Then fell shy of the gas pedal by about a foot. *Brazil and his mile-long legs*. Franco searched for a lever to slide the seat... "Oh. Electric..."

"Good morning, Bobby."

"Dafuck..."

"What would you like to listen to?" continued the disembodied voice.

"Uhh... Uhh..."

"Playing 'Uhh Uhh' by Young Jeezy."

"No... Ay. Excuse me, Robot Lady..."

No dice.

Franco put the Suburban in reverse. Looked back. Two booster seats... A basket of books...

In Franco's 360 backup glancings, the screen also caught

his eye. The central one just below the dash. Showing the Suburban in reverse. Franco reacted with the wonderment of the double rainbow guy. As Young Jeezy dropped a quadruple nigga. Young Jeezy who was also... *celebrating* CTE?[11]

Franco cruised Woodbridge's downtown. The overhaul of the train station area underway. New condominiums to put population density at a maximum. Attract yuppies that didn't wanna pay Manhattan prices. Or Hoboken or Jersey City or Westfield prices for that matter. *Woodbridge: The Goodwill of yuppie housing.*

Franco pulled into the driveway of Brazil's classic colonial. One of them houses in The Wood made of hundred-year-old wood. But. The exterior was freshly painted. Same for the white gate running along the wraparound porch. A swinging chair hanging there amid redone windows and doors. Classic yet modern. Like if George Washington was gonna stay in Woodbridge again, he'd knock on Brazil's door.

Franco meanwhile settled for a honk. The Bogans brood bolted out—

Backpacks bobbing on Mayra, Noelle, and the twins: Robert and Robin.

The original plan was for Bobby (Brazil) and Brenda to have two kids. Hopefully a boy then a girl, Brazil admitted to Franco during a mat session way back. As he flattened Franco on his back. Brazil had quoted that line from that high school book... *The best-laid plans of mice and men often go awry.* But Franco reversed Brazil before he could get his full mount, didn't he? While thinkin of Baby T. *Yeah, sometimes they go better,* Franco had fired back. Back when Young Franco and

---

[11] Franco would later learn from Joey that Jeezy meant it as Corporate Thug Entertainment.

Julie wouldn't let anyone take their miracle for a mistake.

Franco exhaled. *Talk about back in the day.* When was the last time Franco had told his boy he'd brought them so much joy? Shit. Not since the kid became a big brother to Kyd. The little ones suck up every free ounce of energy don't they? Like the ones running his way–

The 10-year-old twins, Robert and Robin. Charging with glee to the SUV–

"Mr. Francooo!" hooted Robert with punches and kicks.

"Let's gooo!" shouted Robin with a spin-kick combo.

Freshman Mayra right behind them. "Hi, Mr. Franco!"

And last but never least, seventh grade Noelle. Who loved to give 'im hell... "Mr. Franco! Thanks for being our Uber driver!"

"You must be gettin lessons from Joey again." Oh. Joe... Franco was gonna have to let him know. Brazil was runnin the show...

"Be quiet, Noelle," urged Robert as he buckled into his booster seat. "Mr. Franco could beat up anybody!"

"Not anymore. He's old."

"Ay Mayra," began the man in question. "Who won the Super Bowl MVP way back in 2002?"

Mayra looked up–jogged her memory faster than Allyson Felix– "Tom Brady."

"How bout all these years later in 2015?"

"Once again... Tom Brady."

Noelle rolled her eyes.

"But he did lose to Eli twice," added Mayra. "Hashtag just sayin just sayin."

"Hashtag G-men," added Noelle as she fist bumped big sis.

Shit could always cut either way, thought the driver cutting the wheel. "Alright where am I droppin yous off?"

"The high school."

"The middle school."

"Ross Street."

"Claremont."

"Four schools?" Franco raised four fingers. Then glanced back– *"Ain't yous twins?"*

"I have gifted and talented today," replied Robin.

"Err I have gifted and talented today," mocked Robert.

"Ya know I'm supposed to be trainin over here. And your dad's got me Driving Miss Daisy."

"Who?"

"Isn't that like some old person movie?" asked Mayra.

"Mr. Franco watches granny movies! Mr. Franco watches granny movies!" chanted the little ones.

The disgruntled captain at the helm let out a long exhale. Like he was Ahab. Chasing a whale...

"Can we fuckin fight now?" huffed Franco as he barged into Brazil's office.

"I'll be right with you, Herc."

"Real fuckin funny." Franco stewed as Brazil kept his bifocals focused on his laptop... "There was a lot of fuckin traffic this morning, you know..."

Brazil finished up. Looked up.

As Franco continued... "Both on the way here and to the eight million schools your kids go to."

"That's some quality family time right there. Did they play 20 questions with you?"

"No, they played break my balls in 20 places..."

"You can't handle kids? How are you gonna handle Basayev?"

"Your kids got a lot more brains than Basayev."

On one hand, Bobby Brazil was a Jiu-Jitsu master playing it straight. On the other, he was a proud papa who let out a split-second smile– But back to the former– "They don't fight as well, though."

"Let's fuckin get ready then."

Brazil got up with an assertive energy that matched the intensity of Franco's f-bomb-filled anger. "Let's do it."

"Okay great. Finally..."

Brazil and his long legs slinked out of the office–

And right into the annex–

He held the door for Franco...

Franco stepped into the dark room. Windowless. Matted wall-to-wall. More mats on the walls. All green save for the battery-operated candles lining the room. The mood they set matching the spiritual melody on the surround sound. Matching the mood of the person already in the room. In some sorta yoga pose with her legs crossed. Palms up. Her white gi dangling from her wrists. As she mumbled something over and over to herself. As her long, dark hair fell all over herself.

Franco knew of Nina. The gym's prodigy. Her multi-sport pedigree. The Latin-Asian now channeling it all into the Latin-Asian art. Kinda like how Steve Nash became the NBA's MVP. By using soccer skills to slash every D.

Brazil raised a finger to Franco, *One second.*

Nina finished up. Stood up. Five-ten flat foot. Bunned her hair with chopsticks. Stepped over.

"Franco. Meet Nina."

The stocky fighter shook hands with the woman. The woman an inch taller...

With a reach longer...

An age younger...

"Maybe you should fight Basayev."

"These hands," said Nina as she held them up–

"Ah right, like De Niro in *Raging Bull*. Bone structure is what it is. Not like these mitts I got." Franco balled his big fists.

"I was going to say... These hands have enough to worry about on the Jiu-Jitsu circuit."

"Oh yeah I don't if Brazil told you... but I'm half a fuckin idiot."

"Well. Hopefully the other half's genius."

Brazil nodded–*we'll see*–and slinked off.

Franco meanwhile clocked Nina's dark hair. Like Julie's... Big browns. Like T's... Pinched at the corners. Like Kyd's... Then her nose. Nothing like Franco's. Hers perfectly straight. Neat at the nostrils. While Franco's flared into a honker. One he subconsciously pinched...

As the twentysomething clocked him likewise. Saw family resemblance likewise. But was it good or bad? That he *looked like her dad*. Her father Paolo back in São Paolo. His body too broken down to follow his *lindeza* around. Nina's Asian-Brazilian mom meanwhile following in *her* parents' footsteps. Keeping the migration moving to America. Right alongside Nina and BJJ at-large. Their new homeland now even home to the world championships. The ones Nina won last summer. The ones she won... *so she could work with this guy?*

Nina put her hands in *Anjali mudra* (prayer) position. Closed her eyes for a mindful moment. To remind herself that he was a *former champion*. Who last won with a *Jiu-Jitsu submission*. Against *The Prince*. Nina had even studied that winning move herself. A move she could right then visualize...

She then opened her eyes...

Nope. Still older. Still heavier.

"So we startin with some Jiu-Jitsu? Not for nothin, but I

got a bit of weight on you. And Basayev's got even more..." noted Franco.

"We're starting with mindful yoga."

"Mindful what? Is this like how John Wooden started with—"

"—teaching his players to tie his shoes."

"You're familiar with UCLA basketball?"

"I *played* UCLA basketball."

Another reminder to Franco. As if the success of Brazil's academy with its day-in day-out classes wasn't enough. He had also attracted talent from all over the country, check that, all over the world. Meanwhile Franco plucked his gym's star outta the local trailer homes. His star that had just exploded into a supernova. While Brazil's prodigy was winning over n over...

"Lotus position," commanded Nina with a point to where Franco could park his ass...

The old man creaked into the spot like his old Mustang at the Meadowlands.

He watched Nina wrap her legs like a fuckin Wetzel's pretzel. Then pulled on his own feet like they were loaded levers... "The ankles. Ain't my strongest part."

"All the more reason to work on them." Nina stretched her arms up—palms up—clasped. All literally straight above her head. No slight bend at the elbow. Nothin.

Meanwhile Franco and his fuckin crab claw arms... *And what the fuck did any of this have to do with going blow for blow with Basayev?*

"Close your eyes. Breathe." Nina modeled: Slow. Through the nose. Out the mouth. She also returned her hands to *Anjali mudra* position before her chest. To give Franco a rest. The lotus alone enough of a test. "Let's set an intention."

An intention? Oh Franco had an intention! To walk out the fuckin door! Half a mind to conduct a camp of his own... But. The breathing. The closed eyes. Parted his mind's skies. Franco had come to Brazil... *because he was wise.* And right in that... *mindful...* moment, Franco couldn't exactly articulate it. But he could feel it. Brazil havin him cart his kids around. Now havin him train with Nina. Maybe Brazil wasn't bitchin him around for the fuck of it. Maybe Brazil was pullin some Jedi mind shit. Some Daniel son paint the fence shit. Franco, legs pretzeled, hands in prayer position, tried to think about it further. But got stuck on wonderin what kind of philosophical question is, *Is Brazil bitchin me around for the fuck of it?* to begin with?

"What the FUCK are you doing?"

It was as if the confused conclusion was spoken out loud. *Cuz it was.* By Franco's best bro. Joey Yo. Standing at the door with boxing gloves slung over his shoulders.

Between being late then bussing Brazil's brood around and now Nina holding court, Franco had lost track of time. Lost track of the fact that he told Yo he should be good for a throw...

"This is a closed class." Nina darted to the door.

Franco unpretzeled. "If you can give us a sec..." Franco added a "Please."

Nina stood her ground with her arms behind her back. Nodded for the two to take it out of her space...

The big-shouldered buds filled into the small hall.

"Let's get in the ring already. I gotta get you ready for some bombs from Basayev. I even started takin steroids!"

Franco was triangulated... Joey in front. Brazil in the office behind. Nina in the annex to his side. Like a thorn in his side. But maybe the prick... needed the prick...

"Joey. I appreciate all that. I've had the same thoughts

108

myself." Franco gestured a hand from his head to Joey's. "But where have our ideas gotten us over the years?"

Joey put his hands on his hips. Pursed his lips. Listened to Franco list...

"In Mulligan's office for bookieing bets in middle school. Then Diaz's office for drivin a Hummer into the high school. Then in our 20s at a bar in New York City. Fightin the New York Mets." Franco put his hands out. "You see what I'm sayin here?"

"Yeah I see what you're sayin. I'm good enough to ride shotgun and shotgun beers. But when it's time for the call up, you call me out to the woodshed instead." Joey shot the boxing gloves into Franco's chest. "Find another buffoon to break your head." The big man's force forced Franco into a backpedal–

Franco caught himself on Brazil's door–

Watched Joey storm the other way.

Franco's chest pounding from the chest pounding. "You got any words of encouragement?"

Brazil gave Franco a couple glances from behind his glasses. Then. "I can get you back on Bunns Lane."

"What?" exhaled Franco.

"Your program. Three-a-days. Six trips back and forth. I mapped Branchton. It's too far." Brazil took his glasses off. "You didn't think about that?"

"Thought I'd crash at Joey's..."

"The best laid plans of mice and men..."

Franco hung on Brazil's use of the old phrase. Was he gonna leave it at awry? Or put Franco's old twist on it? Of course Brazil couldn't give Franco the satisfaction either way. Franco had half a mind to call him out on it. But... He closed his eyes. Took a *mindful* breath. His other half a mind realized Brazil wasn't even sure himself if the Bunns Lane plan would go well. Only time would tell...

"They've relocated everyone from your old building. It's next on the chopping block. I can get you in for the next month or so."

Wow. Six weeks and Franco's childhood home was gonna get the wrecking ball. As half of Bunns Lane had gotten already. New housing upshot in the demo'd spots already... As Franco stood there. In little more than underwear. Without his best bro. When he last talked to T... he didn't know. Readying for his return to The Show. As his fight club readied for close. And here was Brazil. Sending him to his childhood home...

"Remember Willy Momo? From maintenance?" continued Brazil. "He'll give you a key–"

"I still got my old one," shot the old one.

On his blow between sessions, Franco blew threw urban to suburban to rural Jersey. Packed a bag...

Then boomeranged to Brawlers. Made a pact with Julie...

"Six weeks. And bye-bye Bunns Lane forever."

Julie broke from the screen saying they were broke. Her husband for once in the office without any jokes... "Still have your old key?"

Franco pulled it from his pocket. The one with the Yankee logo. Rusted long ago.

"You'll need cage time."

"We're gonna get started on Bobby's mats today. But yeah, probably wrap three-a-days here." Franco motioned out to the empty cage. "If you can spare it..."

Julie looked out at the gym at-large. Empty save for a

lone puncher sputtering the speed bag. "Think I can work it out."

"*Think?*" Franco likewise looked out at the lone puncher. Then back to Julie. Always so focused on her big blues... he'd missed her little smile...

"Think you're the only one that can tell jokes?"

"You wanna fight Basayev too?"

"That one's all you."

Franco dropped a defeated fist on the desk. Then smiled as he met Julie at the side of it.

The two embraced in the overstuffed space.

Jewels looking up at Franco's face...

"You got us in this mess..."

Franco had to check for the smile. Then played back–
"How much for the cage time?"

"More than you can afford."

Franco moved in for a smooch... "I can pay in other ways..."

"That's okay. I take layaway."

"Oh, I can lay away..." confirmed Franco as he went for the jugular. Planted a kiss on it...

The two tripped over boxes.

Fell to the floor.

The speed bagger watching...

As Julie shut the door.

After two of his three-a-days were done. When the fighter was completely done. He still had the biggest one. The third and final session of every day. After all the mindfulness and yoga. All the strength and conditioning. All the technical skills drills. Franco lying on his back trying to escape Brazil's mount. Twisting and gripping–but always down for the count. A little brother smothered. And just when Franco was ready to call it a night...

Get out there and fight. With a 200-pound killer who's fresh. While Franco's a mound of exhausted flesh. A triathlete on his last legs. Guttin out the last leg. *While taking punches and legs.*

"Outquick. Outstick," began Brazil on that first day. As he stood on his mats looking out at Main. Before Franco, Nina, Taz... *and Ray.* "Forget ground and pound. Basayev already won that matchup once. Tack on two championship rounds and 15 pounds... it would only be worse."

Franco did his best not to shrug his sculpted shoulders.

"We'll be more limber. More mindful." Brazil nodded to Nina. "We'll have more angles..."

"Eighteen squared," tallied Taz. The squad's shorthand for noting the infinite amount of MMA moves available. Eighteen standing for the 18 ways you could attack *with your lead arm alone.* The jab, the hook, the over, the hammer, the uppercut, the various elbows. All of those to the head. *And* to the body. The squared denoting that you could combine those 18 moves with 18 moves *for the lead leg alone.* And once you factored in all the combinations with the power arm and power leg, you were already damn near approaching infinity. *Before you even got to the grappling.* Wrestling, Jiu-Jitsu, Krav Maga. The fighter playing keys like Gaga.

Those keys that were all fresh on Franco's brain from helping Ray train. Yeah the kid got turned in early in his last fight. But the moves the kid had in his arsenal? Franco'd ready for him like Chelsea for Arsenal. Monday through Friday for five years. As Ray brought his 18-squared and beyond. Damn did it lean Franco up. Quicken Franco up. Dancing on the canvas like it was laced with hot coals. As Ray kept coming with throws. Franco having to hang in and counter the blows. Keep the kid on his toes.

All of that *after* a full year of Franco rehabbing the ankle. Properly. Not like when Franco was in his 20s and in a hurry. Afraid his career would be buried.

All in all, Franco was now 41 and feeling terrific. Like he was Tom Terrific. The aging Patriots quarterback still terrific. Cuz ever since that day... when Franco met Ray... Franco had seen his best fitness and focus yet. A hustling vet training his all-in bet. Yeah Franco was a shitty gym owner. And take your pops on him as a pops. But he *never* brought less than a hundred percent to the cage. For better or worse, it was his life's stage. But. They hadn't talked, Franco and Ray. Couldn't find the words to say...

But here was Brazil on the camp's first day... "Franco. Do you need a world-class 185er to spar with?"

World-class. Franco so busy starin into the abyss all the time, he couldn't see the mountain built up before him. Sure, Ray had a bad night. A bad fight. *But the kid was 23 and already ranked 23.* Yet one little bump and Franco's all down in the dumps. Thinkin him and Ray chumps. Now here was Brazil and his brazilliance. With his question's hidden message: RESILIENCE.

Franco nodded. "No doubt."

"Ray. You quittin the fight game on us any time soon?"

"No sir."

Sir! Franco dragged the kid outta the trailer park. Turned him into a contender. *And he never once called Franco sir!* But... Franco didn't make a stir. Instead, he looked around the academy at the awards and photos. Showcasing *all* from the dojo. What was hung up at Brawlers? Pictures of Franco's own ass.[12] Franco's head too far up his own ass. So what did

---

[12] Not like nudes or nothin like the kids are sendin these days.

Franco, standing under Brazil's sign, expect? The one that read: *GIVE RESPECT. GET RESPECT.*

"Then let's go." Coach nodded at Ray n Franco.

They shook hands. Squared off.

The sparring session had begun.

As Franco circled the mat.

A square one.

TRACK 12. INTERLUDE / FOR BILLY

TJ FELL ASLEEP NEXT TO HIS NOTEBOOK. All night it took...

Dear Billy,

This one's for you...

Billy Joel, Sandra Day, Crimea, John McCain
Michael Jackson, Dave Chappelle, Janet Super Bowl
Taylor Swift, UFC, Obama, Dick Cheney
Electric cars, flights to Mars, one million TV shows

Gitmo, smart bombs, Howard Stern, Tiger Mom
Syria, Cali wine, every child wins a prize
Amazon, amphetamines, Portland's got a new scene
Red states, Antifa, Robin Williams goodbye

The world's still on fire
Higher burning
As the world keeps turning

The world's still on fire
No we didn't start it
But we poured gas on it

Elton John Rocket Man, Kim Jong Rocket Man
Al Gore, Michael Moore, country's the new rock
Neo-Nazis, snowflakes, bullying, safe space
Muammar Gaddafi falls, we all love The Rock

Rousey, Weinstein, Chicago's got a winning team
Harry Potter, Lieutenant Dan, Bruce Springsteen, Neverland
Bill Clinton, Plastic, Florida, Cruise ships
Princess Kate, Will & Grace, Oxy in the coal hills

The world's still on fire
Higher burning
As the world keeps turning

The world's still on fire
No we didn't start it
But we poured gas on it

Silicone, Beyoncé Knowles, Elon Musk, Twitter trolls
ISIS, Columbine, How did Jon Benét die?
BP spill, gun bill stall, Minnesota mega mall
Mayweather, Russian brides, Rwandan children genocide

Oprah Winfrey, ban fur, Malala, cancer
Ice caps, cornhole, Romney is a no-go
Putin, tuition fees, Hillary and Benghazi
Kardashian, Morning Joe, politics on late shows

The world's still on fire
Higher burning
As the world keeps turning

The world's still on fire
No we didn't start it
But we poured gas on it

Fifty Shades, Sully lands, OJ Simpson takes the stand
Kendrick, Netflix, Schieffer Face The Nation
Hijackers from Arabia, Cena Wrestlemania
Sandberg, Tyson, Megyn versus Anderson
Pope Francis, Brad's ex, closet politician sex
Kurt Cobain blown away, world's burning anyway!

The world's still on fire
Higher burning
As the world keeps turning

The world's still on fire
No we didn't start it
But we poured gas on it

Selfie sticks, action flicks, George Bush back again
Legal pot, Tupac, Whitewater, Hip-Hop
9/11, iTunes, beheadings on YouTube
Nuke deal in Iran, Iraq and Afghanistan

BLM, ADD, mumble rap, Hey Siri
Motel kids, private jets, VR sex, no-aid vets
Refugees on the shore, border's under martial law
Identity and Info Wars
Who can take it please no more!

The world's still on fire
Higher burning
As the world keeps turning

The world's still on fire
And as we live on
It will burn on
Until it's all gone

The world's still on fire
Higher burning
As the world keeps turning

The world's still on fire
No we didn't start it
But we poured gas on it

Much Love,

TJ

TRACK 13. GHETTO SUPERSTAR

FRANCO. IN A PRIVATE, CANDLE-LIT ROOM. With an attractive girl. That did nothin but tweak his body and torture his brain. And why did he call her a girl even though she was in her 20s? The things he thought about for 40 days. Forty days of her remindin him to be mindful. Mindful as his ankles screamed for help. Mindful as he bent backwards into camel pose. Mindful as he was ordered to search inside his heart n soul. *He'd have a good look at both when he snapped in half.*[13]

But over each hour, Franco would eventually get lost in deeper thoughts. It was some time in plow position where he plowed through the guilt of Nelly's death. Yeah, Franco's actions may have technically led to it. But Franco's moves had no malice. The opposite actually. Period.

It was posing in warrior when Franco declared himself a warrior. One that would fight until he could fight no more. Whether that was one fight or ten more. And it was in plank when Franco vowed to walk the plank. Serve any sentence life gave him post-fight game. Stay-at-home dad. Or back

---

[13] Franco imagines his soul as, like, a glowin ball inside his left ab.

down the docks. For once, pile up some stocks. For once, plan ahead. Or as he transitioned to the more creative *Bhujapidasana*, Franco thought up an even more creative future. *Never* leave the fight game. Entertain the fans as a personality. A win would guarantee that. The short list of two-belt champs were Show royalty. *Internationally known* as that old song told him all along: "It Takes Two." Damn was Franco's mind makin connections– *Like he was T–*

Franco opened his eyes. Broke from the darkness.

"Eyes closed."

How did Nina even know? *Her* eyes were closed. In any case. Franco rose. "Had enough for this morning is all."

"That's exactly when you need more. Come on. Into championship rounds."

Franco sighed. The young lady in lotus reminding him of the extra rounds tacked on title bouts. The need to push till ya barely know your whereabouts. But all this thinkin... was wearin him out. "I'll put in some extra training."

The exiting fighter made two fists.

Nina's hands on her hips...

And Franco did come alive every training day. Like he was Denzel in *Training Day*. And the mornings after? Football players talk about how the day after a game feels like a car crash. *That was with helmets and pads. Once a week.* Franco in training? Punished *every day*. Like he was ten all over again. Punches to the face. Wrenchings of the neck that mashed his molars into his tongue. Left him talkin like that flagpole kid in *A Christmas Story*. Chokes of the throat an even worse story. And Franco would straight-up shiver. From knees to the kidneys, kicks to the liver. And after all those hits? Crashes to the canvas. Gettin dragged around till your scalp burns and your ears throb. Followed by contortions of epic proportions. A tortured martial artist. But you're in it. In the moment. A pro training for The Show. Achieving what Nina calls *flow*.

The mornings after, though. Sore in places you didn't know. Muscle recovery? That was easy. Try bruised bone. Lacerated ligaments. Scathed skin. Crushed cartilage. Your body crushed. Like Carthage. Unable to roam.

But. *This camp was different.* Franco would wake up. Give his body a mindful minute. Then swing his legs from the edge. Ready for pain to shoot from the balls of his feet. Making the toilet a worthy feat...

But each morning as Franco tiptoed... ready for pain with its own zip code... it never showed. At least not to the level of the fighter's camps back in the day. Now first thing in the morning and... *Franco could touch his toes. Wiggle his nose. Felt so good, he'd even rip a few throws.*

Because of Nina. Because of a health regimen as terrific as Tom Terrific's. And. Because of the last five years of Ray's fists rubber stamping him. And now it was Franco's turn to go on the offensive. Dish it out with no reservations like he was Anthony Bourdain.

Franco. In flow.... Five am and wantin to be awake...

Bustin out of his old apartment in a hurry to bust up Ray. Runnin a hand through his hair on his way. Fuck his gray. For each one, ten black. For all his personal gripes, call him Snipes. *And bet on black.* Sprinting each morning to the mats. Gettin mindful. Settin intentions. *And damn how he was stretchin...*

Then running Brazil's latest invention. The customized grappling game of counters and quickness. The bigger Brazil, standing in for Basayev, goes for a high mount, Franco escapes low. Brazil goes for a throw, Franco goes with it. Rides the momentum and wraps around. Turning from total weakness to total strength–at his opponent's back and ready to attack. Then the submission holds. Brazil breaking Franco's habit of trying to power out of them. As the smaller, faster guy, he was gonna slip them. Or again, go with them. Ride them further than Basayev expects. With Franco's new ability to stretch. Let The Beast wear down. *Then turn on the jets...*

Taz was the main man for that feat. Cooking up combos more savory than Combos. Calf kick to throw off Umar–throw out a half-inch opening–split his forearms–split his lip. Follow-up to the body with the power hand. Take control and finish the man. Taz instructing Franco on every angle's precision. Franco needing perfect strikes to take the decision. But. Taz was a bantamweight. Shorter. Smaller. Sure, Franco could manage the angle adjustments better than when he was a sophomore putzin around with a protractor. But still... Off by an inch and he'd miss the kill. So there was that issue. Franco was hesitant to bring up with Brazil...

Franco took a breath. Approached...

Brazil on the side mat. The master belting out jacks. "What's up?"

"I was thinkin. Doin a lot of thinkin actually..." Franco motioned over to the annex. "Anyway, I was thinkin I gotta get Joey back. 'Case this thing turns into a slugfest."

Brazil stood tall as he broke from his jacks. Like he was the giant and Franco was Jack. "Man this ain't gonna be no slugfest..."

Franco always knew when Brazil was gettin heated. When he started talkin street. "Joey could at least get me ready for some big hits. I mean, I'll try to avoid em. But Basayev ain't exactly gonna go along with our plan..."

Brazil craned his head down. The giant down to have a word with Jack. "And what's *your* plan? To let Joey smash you up? Send you into the fight half punch drunk. Then let Basayev finish the job. Send you punch drunk into the rest of your life," surmised Brazil as he motioned to Main Street. *"Man that ain't tough! Any fool can get his head smashed in!"* Brazil stuck his cigar-sized finger into Franco's forehead. "You don't ever give up on this. You master this." The Phillies finger then motioned to Main. "Then you master the world." Brazil was in tight. Lowered eye-to-raised eye with Franco. *Whatchyou gonna do...*

Franco had half a mind throw a clip straight from the hip. Street style. Like the two were back on Bunns Lane. But his other half a mind... told him to breathe. *Kindly communicate*, as Nina would say. Or that Spanish saying she loved. *Por las buenas.* How if you gotta tell someone some shit, do it in the nicest way possible. And Franco had a lotta shit to tell his head coach. Shit he'd discovered in this new approach. In the annex meditating. His mind elevating. So he laid out to Brazil what he'd realized laid out in bridge position...

Everyone in the world had their talent. Yeah maybe Joey was a bit immature. A bit uneducated. A bit easily agitated. But all that could be said about Franco too, couldn't it? And couldn't it be, that in the right situation, Joey was more brilliant than that kid that invented Facebook? Joey studied *everything* about boxers. Failed eighth grade science but had mastered the sweet science. Franco was the mixed martial artist. But the boxing component? *Yo owned it.* A game of inches within a game of inches. A fine line between Mad Max and Greg Maddox. Gone insane or Hall of Fame. Hands up. Chin tucked in. Don't go for any big blocks. Leaves ya open to get clocked. All tight. Precision. Deflect just enough. Stay in position. *Swoosh. Swoosh.* Windshield wiping. *Tight. Fast.* All while countering. The mind somehow slowing it down while the hands worked at turbo. Slow and fast like that snail in *Turbo*. Yeah Joey (and Franco) would see nothin but ones and zeroes on some computer codin screen or some shit. But watchin boxing? Mark Zuckerman[14] wouldn't see if a fighter was flarin his elbow out too much on straights. Cockin back too much on power shots. *Torque from the torso. Pop.* Wouldn't see if pacing one way or the other affected an opponent one way or the other. Wouldn't see if a fighter's defense cheated toward his head or body. Or if his arms wore lower as the fight wore on. Greg Maddox never had the power of the big boys. The Randy Johnsons, the Roger Clemenses, the Nolan Ryans. But. *He retired with more wins than all of them.* Cuz he mastered that fine line between ball and strike...

"That's what Joey could help me do. Master the difference between block and strike. I mean, he's even the same size as Basayev. And nah I don't want him to bash my head in. I want him to help me avoid that." As Franco stood before Brazil, he felt his work in the annex annexing his mind. On the surface makin him more kind. But inside, strengthenin his spine. Even gave him the fortitude to add, "And not for nothin, he knows a thing or two about strength and conditionin..."

Brazil's spine at least as strong as his stare continued...

"And..." Franco's final *and* just kinda came out. As if forced out by Brazil's bronze eyes. As if it had occurred to Franco that maybe there was a deeper reason yet to bring Joey back. One Franco couldn't even... *what the fuck was that word Nina kept using...* access. "I dunno. Just feels like the right thing to do. And I wanna do it."

"Alright then. Bring him back," the giant said to Jack.

---

[14] Zuckerberg. *Come on Franco.*

Then got back to his jacks.

"Okay," concluded Franco. Made his way from master to main entrance. "Oh. Also."

Brazil broke from his jacks as Franco broke more news...

"Saturday afternoon to Monday morning, I'm off the grid. Gonna spend the time with Julie n Kyd."

Brazil chewed on it. Nodded, *You got it.*

Franco made his way out onto Main. Out into the world. With half a mind to look back. To see if Brazil was irked... He woulda seen.

Head coach smirked.

Franco knocked on the door of unit 204. Heard some loud *OHHHs*. Banged harder.

Joey swung the door open. Gave a much lower, "Oh."

"Watchin the fights from last night?"

"Nah, The Challenge," began Joey. Then with a sheepish shrug, "Battle of the Exes."

Franco poked his head in. Saw Herc on the couch...

"Season Two! Bananas is back!" shouted the schlub eatin a sub. Ham hangin from his mouth.

Joey stepped halfway outside. Brought the door halfway shut. "What's up?"

"I been thinkin. It ain't that you ain't good enough to be a head trainer. It's just, we're too the same you n me. Mixed martial arts. It's like... I gotta diversify."

"Fuckin Charles Schwab over here."

"If you were still boxin, I wouldn't want ya to hire me to head coach either."

Joey chewed on it like Herc on his ham. "So, how is the camp goin?"

"Good. I mean... pretty good. It's missing one big fuckin

piece, though. Like a big... 200-pound piece."

Joey nodded. Then stepped all the way out. "Let's do it."

"Just like that? Everything I said makes sense?"

"Nah I'm just sick of fuckin hangin out with Herc." Joey started for the stairs. "Let's get to work!"

Franco followed... "You're just gonna leave him at your place?"

"Can't get rid of the guy. He's like herpes."

"That's what you should start callin him. Herces."

Joey bust out laughing as they beat feet out to the street. "God I fuckin missed you!" cried Yo. As he threw an arm around his bro.

"Whadayasay now, WOOD!" hollered a homegal from the passenger seat of a Plymouth.

Joey shot back, "Whadayasay now, WOOD!"

Franco and Joey continued past the corner store. The one they'd known since four...

"I said, *Wood...*" barked Joey out the side of his mouth.

"Bridge," returned Franco.

"I said, Wood..." gutted Joey through gritted teeth.

"Bridge."

"I said, WOOD!" Joey bellowed from his belly.

"And I said, BRIDGE!" fired Franco.

The two strutted all in a lurch. As they passed that old church... *Nelly's. Woodbridge's first...*

"WOOD!"

"BRIDGE!"

"WOOD!"

"BRIDGE!"

"Where you from Basayev?" Joey called as he strut down the street.

"Cuz I'm from The Wood bitch. Hood bitch. Woodbridge!" hooted Franco.

Joey hopped around. Slapboxed at Franco.

Franco had gotten his mind right in lotus...

And now Joey had him on "Otis." Franco's swagger back as he went on the attack. Cuz he was no longer going through the camp alone. Now on some Kanye & Jay–some *Watch the Throne*. The homeboys slapboxin in the street–gettin after each other. A modern day Mantle & Maris. On some "Niggas in Paris."

Watch the Throne. That album they played the whole camp. A warning to the champ. Cuz Brazil had Franco re-styled. Nina had his head mild. Taz gave his angles guile. Ray–cardio for miles. And Joey. Above all. Gave him the joy of a child.

But even with the whole camp clicking all day every day...

It was the night. That was the real fight. Franco had once heard Seinfeld say something about how, in pickin a career, you should pick the torture you enjoy most. Franco had signed up for the torture of the days. The nights. Not so much. Starting with the very first one back on Bunns...

The key Franco had as a kid still worked. And still got stuck. Now even worse with the rust.

The light switch at the entrance of his project apartment also worked. Only now it turned on a red bulb dangling from the ceiling like a mic from haunted rafters. *In this corner, a man who's no stranger to this hole. A man who lived here decades ago. Now back for one more go. Fran-cooooo!* The event attendees? Cucarachas doing "La Cucaracha" on molded enchiladas n Sriracha. The place *way* worse than when Franco's old man used to blast Sinatra. At least after Franco's old man smashed up the walls all plastered, the next day, he'd make sure they got plastered. Some of his old man's old spackle jobs still on display. On the white walls he smoked gray. The ones that were red tonight. His old man gladly dead tonight. The site of his old place. He'd put that classic look on his face. And say. *What a fuckin disgrace.*

Franco stepped onto carpetless pink padding that always reminded him of human insides. One of the few things unremoved from inside. Along with the olive table still back there. In the "dining" area. Where Franco's old man dined on boxed wine. The table square to fit in the square room. Riveted to the floor. A feature that came in handy when Franco's old man would smash it. Bitch about how the lack of a rectangle wrecked a man's pride. *Could they have at least went with round like the Knights of the Round Table? Of course not. Just a fuckin square! Tellin me I'm a square! In this two-bedroom dump the shape of a square. Or whatever the hell it is, a cube. A fuckin cage at the zoo.* Then to Young Franco... *It's a hell of a life, little dude.* Then raise his fuckin glass. *Salud.*

Franco passed the stairs over his left shoulder as he moved from living area to dining area. The entered the kitchen tucked in the back left. The only first floor room left.

Franco entered as a rat left– Booked out the window above the sink. Franco reached to shut that window– Saw a black widow– Recoiled his hand in the nick of time– Nicked the sink. Woke fruit flies that flew in his nose, his ears, his eyes. Sent him into his old fridge. Franco still taller by a smidge. He opened the door. Barely on the hinge. The only thing inside was remnants of cake. Like whoever was here last was eating it by the handful. Franco took a breath. *Tried to be mindful...*

Franco would've preferred mindless, memory-less as he took tepid steps upstairs. Toward the Jack-and-Jill bedrooms. The shared bathroom. His old man's laugh room. Always in there shavin n ravin about some bet. *Pretty soon he'd be drivin a Vette!*

Step by step, stair by stair. Franco breathed staler and staler air. The busted-out kitchen window suddenly the best fuckin feature of the house. Apartment. Project. Whatever. Wait, yeah. Definitely a *project.*

Franco stepped into the ~~upstairs~~[15] bathroom. Whoever ripped off the shower curtain didn't take the time to reattach the rod. At least they left the smashed mirror. The one haunted in the moonlight...

Franco stood before it examining his fragmented reflection. Like John King breakin down an election. In one fragment, Franco's brushed-to-the-side hair was longer and grayer than ever. *Like he was his old man.* In another, the gaze of his hazels. *His head in a fog over seein The Frog.* But. Franco's eye shape had more pizazz. Kinda like Nina n Taz. And Franco's honker nose... was just like Joey Yo's. And all of that was atop Franco's wide mouth. Yeah, he was lookin just like Brazil to the south. And when Franco held his receded hair back, he had to laugh from his belly. *He looked just like Nelly!*

The old man stepped into his old man's room. Franco thought seeing it bare bones would be an upshot. But the gutted room... *was a gutshot...*

Franco moved to the last spot. Thought its emptiness would uplift him without a doubt. A reminder... *He'd made it out.* Until it hit him and his duffel bag slung over his shoulder. Here he was, once again over. For 40 days and 40 nights. He pressed the switch. But it didn't light.

Franco took a seat against the bare wall. Looked out the bare windows. Across the street. His first house. With his

---

[15] *The only fuckin bathroom in the place. Upstairs! A fuckin disgrace! -Franco's old man circa... circa every fuckin day of Franco's childhood.*

first family. Him. Julie. T...

Then Tonio Franco Senior shifted left, shifted right. But just couldn't sit right. And he wasn't about to get up either. *Something* had emerged from the ether. *Someone*. At the doorway. A big-shouldered bastard. Shaded darker than the night. Someone who had T's father squirming. Seething...

Cuz there were two Tonio Francos.

And there were two fuckin demons.

TRACK 14. KAMARA CHAMELEON

TJ AND KAMARA LAY ON HER COUCH. Kamara's
thesis turned in. T's interning over. Their senior year almost
over. The two spending most nights with each other.
Dancing with Candi and T's crew to "Sugar, Sugar" at DOG
house parties. Hitting the scene at Maxine's to catch Ruth's
shows. More dinners where they had their first date. They
especially loved going when the weather was "cloudy with a
chance..." But more than any of that. They'd lay on Kamara's
couch. And watch shit TJ would never watch in a million
years otherwise.

Like that night they watched Kamara's favorite movie.
The Iron Giant. That robot wondering who he's supposed to
be. His pal unlocking the mystery... *You are who you choose to be.*
Or when they'd watch *The Daily Show with Jon Stewart*. A few
episodes in and Jon Stewart was added to *both* of TJ's top-
secret lists. Top secret until Kamara tickled them out of him...

"Okay. One is my Jersey Hall of Fame. The other is my...
Superundersized Hall of Fame."

"Super what?"

"It's like... every undersized guy secretly knows. Which

famous guys are his height or less."

Kamara raised her eyebrows. "Gimme your top ten."

"Ooh I never narrowed it down it like that..."

TJ got up. Had to pace the candlelit room. All five-seven of him...

"Lionel Messi. Greatest player in the world's greatest game, thank you very much. Bob Dylan. Greatest songwriter ever. Oh. The three Jersey ones. Jon Stewart. Frankie Edgar. Tom Cruise–"

Off Kamara's crooked look–

"So he jumped on a couch! Can we give the guy a break? He's Jerry Maguire for God's sake!"

Off Kamara's satisfied nod...

"Manny Pacquiao. Kevin Hart. Billy Joel. Ooh and I can't leave out Altuve. No way José!"

"That's nine..." laughed Kamara.

"Already? One left?" TJ put his hands out. "Do you have any idea what kind of rift this could cause in the superundersized alliance?"

"I promise not to Tweet it..."

TJ took a breath. Resumed his pacing. "Well I can't make another mooove. Without pourin one out for Langston Huuughes. And all the OGs. Like Prince. Winston Churchill. Houdini– No wonder he could escape so easily."

Kamara laughed out loud over this crazy boy boy boy.

"And *really* OGs. Like Isaac Newtown and Aristotle. *Contemplate those!*"

Kamara rested her chin on her fist like she was *The Thinker* himself...

"And don't forget to make room and roll over... for Beethoven! Or one that's a real Picasso...

"I know... Pablo!" called out Kamara.

"But back to the living." TJ raised an index. "I could go

with a business icon. Like Daymond John. A superstar. Like Bruno Mars. An international star. Like Sachin Tendulkar. But if I can only pick one more. I gotta go with a rapper..."

Kamara put her hands together in anticipation...

"And if you asked me, even a month ago, which rapper was in my top ten, it would def be Eazy or Weezy..." But as TJ looked at Kamar. He thought of those songs they'd hear at the bars. From the album she always played in her car...

"...but I gotta go. With Kendrick Lamar."

Kamara welcomed TJ to the couch. Cooed into his ear... "Bitch, that definitely didn't kill my vibe."

The two lay thigh to thigh. Eye to eye.

As Kamara killed the lights.

Kicked off her sandals.

Leaving...

Two lovers.

Ten candles.

Other nights, TJ would just lay there. Stroke her hair. Stay hush as *she* gushed. As she told him all about her dad. The racism she'd faced. The quiet kid impressed. All her trauma addressed. *And* she had her future figured out. Anticipating letters from grad school admissions. Researching the human condition her mission...

"You know. Assuming my super-secret fantasy dream doesn't work out," equivocated Kamara.

"Marrying me and having six children?"

The post-coital Kamara laughed. Her caramel body bound only by undergarments as off-white as the topless boy beside her. "Okay my *other* super-secret fantasy dream. Becoming a famous singer. Little pop. Little rap." Kamara buried her face in her hands. "Omg I can't believe I just told you that. Especially when you're actually serious with rap..."

TJ turned on his side. "Well. You said you sang choir..."

"Me and how many million? And it's not like I had to write the songs..."

"Let's hear it."

"Hear what?" Kamara backed her head away.

"Anything. Sing." TJ looked into those goldens. Put a gentle finger on her forehead. "You've got the looks." Ran it down her smooth nose. Over those full lips. Let it fall from the cliff that was her cleft chin. "I know you can write." TJ's finger ran through her valley. Buzzed through peach fuzz. Bumped on her belly button. "And I know you can move these hips. I've got the bruises to prove it."

Kamara looked to TJ. On his side. Gettin lost in her eyes... Then took a breath. Made a face of unrest....

"Ahhmaaazing Grace
How sweet the sound
I once was lost
but now am found."

Kamara exhaled that breath. Her face now at rest.

"That was... ahhmaaazing," sung T. Only way worse.

"Thanks, but I don't see it topping the charts..."

TJ scrunched his face. Once again popped up. Started to pace. Circled the coffee table as he circled his index...

"Yeah it's Kimura
Know you want more-a
But I'm a good girl-a
Go find a whore-a

I'll be on toura

Explorin like Dora
Rock from Iraq
To Bora Bora"

Kamara sat up. "What's... Kimura?"

"A Jiu-Jitsu hold..." TJ tried to find the right words. Explain that she had *him* in one. In a good way. But the reference to MMA... threw off TJ...

Kamara meanwhile leaned forward. "Watch Dora with your sister?"

TJ took a seat at the far edge of the couch. "Summer before we moved. To Branchton."

MMA. The family move... The reminders put T from a peak to a valley. Storm clouds rolling into his head... Like when he was 15. *And hid under his bed.*

Yeah TJ and Kamara would lay on that couch and talk about everything. Except *THE* Thing...

T sprang for the door without warning– "Gotta get up in the morning–"

"Hey– Wait– See you tomorrow night?"

"What's tomorrow night?" asked the kid halfway out the door...

"Ruth wants you to meet the booking manager... For her show... Over at Chester's..."

That old schoolyard phrase. Chester, Chester the child molester...

The shook kid shook his head. "Oh. Yeah. I have it calendared. And alarmed." T patted his pocketed phone. "See you then."

Kamara watched the kid run off. Like he was gonna turn into a pumpkin. *What the hell was up with him? Somethin...*

Oh. And the fucking G-thing. G giving T a needling. Back at

their penthouse's bar. G asking...

"What's up with Sori. What's the story?"

TJ's plan was to hit the hay. Wake up, practice what he'd say. At the interview. The one arranged by the dude before him. The one who implored him—

"Give me something."

TJ had to take a pill. Just one to chill. And sure, a Beast Light wouldn't kill. His interview wasn't till 11 anyway. Right across the way. He could still sleep in. Coffee n ibuprofen. Cruise out of Hoboken. Shit, pop another pill on the ferry and he'd be fuckin merry. *So yeah hang with G like you're fuckin* Tom & Jerry. TJ this whole time mousing around. Evading the cat on the prowl... "What's it matter if Sori and her crew take down the statue anyway?"

G slammed his Beast Light on the bar. Turned down Eminem's "So Far..."

"Are you fucking kidding me? Where does it end? Look what happened to your boy LaCroix!"

Lance. In the room next door. Through the posters of whores. The one with a work station stationed where G and T's bar was. A proper dresser where their plastic crates were. A ground-floor bed while TJ laddered up to a loft. Lance even had a fridge full of food. *Such an organized dude. G was right! What they did to him was rude!*

While TJ was off to JSUH after high school, Lance's lacrosse had lofted him higher. Full ride to Valhurst, one of the top liberal arts colleges in America.

Kid's life was goin great. Until... "Condomgate." Lance's teammate. A one-night date. The undisputed details. The teammate and the girl were out drinking. Then got naked and rounded the bases. First then second. Third, then he took a second. To open a condom box. Open the wrapper. Put it on. And head for home.

Afterward, walked her home.

The now-published texts from their phones:

Hers: *Hey. U couldn't tell I froze? I was too drunk to say no...*
His: *Wut. A month ago?? No I didn't know! I was drunk too yo!*

The local press to the story like vultures...

The national exposé on Valhurst's rape culture...

The social media outcry over the goonery of the lacrosse team at-large. And once debaucherous photos from their parties surfaced... it was a rebuke on par with '06 Duke.

Forget that, as G argued in his online article, the photos were of the garden-variety shenanigans that was happening on every campus in America. *Photos of intoxicated underage kids with underdeveloped brains.* And forget that the pics were yanked out of context. Forget that nothing was proven. As Sori and *her* online article did. As the Valhurst administration did. They closed the lacrosse house and canceled the season. *Because of mob outrage and no other reason!* G's article reasoned. And no, the girl's months-later retraction didn't please him. When she said maybe it was just a bad date. Crumbling the exposé like UVA's. *Yeah sure change your mind. Any time! Don't worry about the lives you destroyed. They're just boys!*

Like the one in the room next door. Lance who, after freshman year, left Valhurst's dog house. Joined TJ at the DOG house. Or as TJ called it back then, the Delta O house. Lance ever since with a plan to be three and out. Pack up and jet quicker than a Jets quarterback. Lance who once vented to T on their way to a tutoring session... *G and his culture war obsession. What was the point? What was the lesson?*

If G would've heard that, he would've grabbed a Smith & Wesson. *When would Lance care? When all men were illegal? Lance a hatchling! Unappreciative of the eagle! And speaking of eagles, they too should be illegal! They must be like doves—less dour! Everything's equal in this fine hour!*

TJ for three years bouncing back and forth listening to G and Lance both. Tied in the middle as they yanked on their ropes. Then along came Kamara. Yanking TJ in yet another direction. Yeah G's Valhurst argument seemed sound. But what about... *The Hunting Ground?* Oh right, G already shot it down! But the general message... Look at Ruth! *Girls had it worse. That was the truth!*

So then why did T... as he drank at the bar with G... think something even more uncouth? Was there an even deeper Truth? TJ's eyes started going REM as he heard REM. "Everybody Hurts." And maybe everybody... *had a Thing*. G and those stories about his mom. Kamara and her dad. And speaking of parents, TJ's dad and all the pain *his* parents fostered. *Paternal and foster.* Maybe... everyone was sad. All the hate drivin everyone mad. Thought T. Pounding beers like Dad. On a dark night back in the day. Son understood now—it lifted the weight. But... Wait. Maybe T... could just tell G. About his Thing! Would that solve anything...

TJ opened his mouth. But the words didn't come out. Like he was the star of "Lose Yourself." *Damn,* he was losin his self!

Thank God for the pill...

The drink refill...

Tell G about The Thing. Ha! Fall from fraternity Vice President to the house's victim resident. Next to Mummy. And Baby. Just for playing "Baby." *One fucking time.* T's Thing a much bigger crime. Fucking G wouldn't even let him hang up a poster of Linkin Park. And T was gonna let *his* secret outta the dark? *Damn T's head was spun...* He slugged another one... "Yeah no I don't know..." *What were we even saying bro!*

"You must know something about Sori... You're over

there *all the time...*"

Yeah TJ was crazy about Kamara. But Sori... *In class so accusatory...*

The mouse made two fists. Threw his lone crumb to the prowling cat before him... "I saw her packing pocket knives. Into riot gear..."

G smiled ear to ear. "Wait until the brothers on the fence hear that. They'll bring *two* bats!" G busted out his own. Patted T on his back. "Happy hour on me after your interview tomorrow."

G swung and swung. Harder and harder.

As T sipped and sipped. Harder and harder.

Till he blacked out...

Woke up on his pleather couch. Under his loft bed. Stood—bumped his head. Like he was the star of "It's Raining, It's Pouring." Then started pouring...

Coffee, Clonium, ibuprofen...

Dashing for the ferry outta Hoboken...

But the fuckin boat...

It was smokin...

TJ ran downtown doing the math... Could still be on-time by taking the PATH...

T's suit jacket flew back like a sail. His man-bag rattled like a rudder. His wooden heels providing the keel under. As up front, his hair bow blew in the breeze. The waters rough, the skiff at full speed...

TJ squeezed onto the PATH train. Train. Ha! Thing was more underground than MF Doom. And in TJ's case, that spelled MotherFuckin doom.

Things TJ had begun avoiding. Ever since the memory came back. To the point of panic attacks. Bridges. Observation decks. Chair lifts–especially grueling when they rock. Over a gorge of rock. Ferris wheels. Roller coasters. Ledges that beckoned T to run over. Fosbury Flop from record-breaking, bone-shattering height. Or go even higher. Open the plane's emergency exit. Gone as psycho as *American Psycho* with no exit. His body tuckered, his brain maxed. Wishing the same thing as Tucker Max. *I Hope They Serve Beer in Hell.* Fuck, even hotel balconies made T weak in the knees. He'd never be able to go away with Kamara. Might as well give her the breeze. They were done anyway once they got their degrees. She off to any school she pleased. While T saw his future like a disease. *Nah he's just kiddin, please. Come on Clonium. Kick in, please! Subways, too, cripple the knees!*

As more suicidal scenarios ran through T's head, he buried his head. To forget that he was in a tin tube. Rumbling through rock. Under a river. Toward where two buildings had been blown up. Amid reminder posters for everyone to keep their head up. But T's was down. Kid doing his best civic part. To not completely come apart.

"Damn," T whispered to himself. Damn, now he was talkin to hisself! Like a real boxcar hobo. Half a mind to jump out and run back to Hobo. Through all the rats and all the water. Run off with Kamara and have a daughter. *For real, he oughta!* His whole life was outta *orda!* Like Al Pacino in that old-ass movie. *...And Justice for All.* The kid so cracked up he was cracking up. Over his take. On the remake. *...And Social Justice for All.* His fleeting laughs leaving a vacancy. For the

urge to scream. Every obscenity. About every identity. Including his own indeed. Like any person wasn't vulnerable to hate to greed. To every evil seed. Like only some bleed... *Hey right here me! The short working-class kid with PTSD. Anyone see... my equity?* But as the nerve-wracked kid took glances around the train... He wondered... *Who on here doesn't feel pain? Doesn't feel strange? Doesn't have reason to file a claim.* Then went wide-eyed over a notion. Passengers from across every ocean... Yet... *All lone dancers at the grand cotillion.* All. *One in seven billion.*

The kid holding the pole turned his earbuds up. *Linkin Park—that's what's up.* Now T could just shut up. Go through his whole life dumb. Just listen to "Numb."

The PATH train pulled into World Trade. T wishing for an alternate life—a world trade. But nah. This was the one he made. No one but himself to thank. *His* choice to save Kyd's house from the bank. But... *what of Dad's latest fight? Bailing his ass out faster than a financial crisis fat cat.* So why was T even pursuing this path? Trudging up from the PATH. Doing double-steps past escalator schleps. *Because he'd come this far.* Four years of acing classes. Interning every summer. *And into senior year.* The leadership and community service. To walk away from it all... would be a disservice...

TJ hurried along the sidewalk. Pressed his man-bag to his hip. Trying to steady his ship. But the breeze still blew his hair bow sideways. Kid coming undone like Haden Church in *Sideways.* Coming undone... but hearing "Carry On" by Fun. Between that and the kicking-in Clonium... *It was kinda fun...*

Until T saw the sun. On the patio of floor 101. *Man it was high in the sky...* T hearing "I Believe I Can Fly." Sung by... *R fucking Kelly.* A tinge in T's belly...

As out walked G's father's colleague. From M & A. The big leagues...

The big leaguer with the big belly. Bald top. Thick brows over gray eyes. Yeah the cuff links and Constantin watch had him looking dapper. But still. *He looked just like T's fucking attacker...*

The big man shook hands with the shook kid.

The shook kid with sweaty palms. Tiptoeing like he'd tripped a bomb. *Come on T, stay calm...*

The big man, *Alfie was it?,* motioned for T to take a seat. On one of them all-weather outdoor couches. As smoke gray as the guy's eyes. *As someone else's eyes...*

"How many nice days per year in New York City?"

TJ had studied every investment banking question in the book. Granted this was a new look. But the same formula. Take the seemingly complex question and chop it into pieces. "I'd say none in January. Or February. Maybe two in March." TJ sat forward. Thought better that way. "Eight in April. Ten-ish May through September. Bell curve it with eight in October, two in November." T was about to sit back– "Wait. Depends how you define nice..."

"GIGO right?" Alfie crossed his arms and spread his legs. Trying to put the kid in limbo with his lingo. His lingo asking T if he knew how important the right assumptions were in setting up a model.

"Yep, garbage in garbage out," said T without flinching. T modeling that *yeah he knew how to fucking model.* Guy should go ask T's old firm. In the middle of an M & A pitch. Based on T's work for Mitch. Who probably took all the credit. *Fucking bi–*

"Warm but not hot. At least some sun. No precipitation. Not too much wind nor humidity," specified Alfie.

"Oh. Zero!"

A laugh from Alfie!

"But really though," continued T. "I was up at 70 on my initial count. I'd have to cut that in half considering all the constraints. But now that feels a little low, so... I'd say 40."

"Thirty-nine."

"Are we playing closest to the answer or Price is Right?" T played back with a playful smile.

"Should have asked beforehand," shot Alfie as he popped forward. His thick eyebrows now shading the sun from his eyes...

"Well, reasonable person standard. These questions are usually closest to the answer..." *Man he looked just like the guy. Man did T wanna get off this ride. Fuckin dyin inside...* And that thing T recently learned in class... Somethin about executive psychopaths. Yeah maybe one day this guy took the PATH. Left his analysts to do the math. As he holed up in Branchton. To have a laugh. Have a little boy's ass. Dressed up like a bum. To leave the county searchin for scum. *God, when's this interview gonna be done!*

"I'm sorry, can you repeat that one?"

"I said. Tell me about a time you've overcome adversity."

Holy shit! T had spaced so hard, he asked the guy to repeat the simplest question. The one to find out if the analyst was willing to work a hundred hours a week no matter what. *Oh you want to stay home with strep throat? Okay, your cubemate'll cut your throat. Take your project and your promotion. Oh you're best man at your buddy's wedding? The same weekend as a merger? Fifty-fifty his merger ends up in divorce anyway. Aw your grandmother died? Don't worry. She won't miss you at the funeral.*

A laugh. Only this time not from Alfie.

From the demon doubling over the patio's edge. He even waved T over. *Come on kid, show's over. Because you heard the question. And you KNOW I'm your answer. Your terminal fuckin cancer...*

T was on the balls of his feet. Eyes darting... *What if HE darted? Like that day. Just lost control and just started running? Only... Right now. Right over the ledge... What if what if what if...*

T blabbed on about how he didn't know any white-collar people growing up. How he had to figure it all out on his own. His hard work. The extracurriculars. The handing out résumés on the street. Maybe it could've all sounded impressive. But the kid. Was so fucking pensive. Blabbing it all with no heart. More concerned. With his racing heart...

TJ rushed out of the building like it was on fire. His head on fire. He crushed a second Clonium– Crashed the bodega below the building– Bought a brown bag 40 for $9.40. And at that ridiculous Manhattan price... *Of course* he picked high-ABV Evil Ice.

Ahh. T feelin nice. Sittin on the ferry. Across from a woman. Sweet as a cherry. Her form-fitting business dress as red as his head. But as the kid sipped his 40... he realized she was at least 40. Shit, she probably had a kid the same age as Kyd. Fuckin beautiful though. Cut calf on stiletto. But that ring. Her wedding bling.

The kid looked to a ship passing...

But kept glancing...

Until he took a breath. Got a whiff of King Kong's latest crap. From the open bathroom door behind him.

T left the woman sweet as a cherry. Headed for the front of the ferry...

Wind flew threw his hair. Kid floatin on air. A captain on-course to Hoboken ahead. *So high,* his altimeter read. As his tachometer pushed into the red. As his speedometer climbed fast. As all compasses. Were completely smashed. For the kid. Completely smashed.

The one hopping over to happy hour so happy. The DJ playing "Happy." And drinks were on that cheap fuck G, even! If T drank a million, they'd be even!

And after a couple, T had so many ants in his pants... he just wanted to dance! Like one of those girls Dane Cook imitates in *Vicious Circle*. The cooked kid living a vicious circle...

As the bar played Kendrick Lamar. "Swimming Pools." T full of liquor and ready to dive in... When G showed him how to turn it up a notch... Ordered two glasses of Scotch. The kid that weighed a buck fifty rocked. Did T even have a brain? Or was it rocks? Kid put a fist to his head. He knocked!

But T'd tell ya one thing. Made him forget all about The Thing. The interview. His future in need of sutures. And... this couldn't be rock bottom. Look at those girls rocking those bottoms! Their little shorts exposing their bottoms! One of their owners pointing at the guy... Saying, *Isn't that Gemini?* A sight for sore eyes! T so high, he was even thankful for ole Lenore. Thanks to her he swore. He'd be exclusive no more! That's right, him and Kamara never made it official. So why not dance to "Whistle"?

Yeah it was all no biggie...

Till she kicked in the door like Biggie.

T lifted his head, dizzy. *What time is it? Where is he?* And... *Is that Kamara? All in a tizzy*...

"To think I was worried about you!"

Oh. He was in his room. And oh– "Just catching a nap–

145

Let's go– It's in my phone–" The half-dressed kid half-fell from his loft–

"This phone?" Kamara picked up the cracked phone from the tiled floor. The cracked phone RINGING over and over...

TJ grabbed it– "Look I have 'Meet K n Ruth' blacked out–" But. That was before he blacked out...

"While you've been 'sleeping' through this alarm, we've already been out! Waiting at Chester's!"

Chester, Chester...

"Watching you on G's Snap story. Taking shots and singing 'Swimming Pools.' *With who knows who...*"

TJ pressed his hands into his face...

As Kamara shoved it in his face... "And by the way, that song is about the *dangers* of drinking!"

"It is?"

"Yeah. It is." Kamara narrowed her eyes. Her goldens *grim* as she grilled him! "Hope it was worth it."

Maybe it was the roaring hangover. Maybe it was the kid's roaring brain. Maybe it was just the day, *the years,* of pain. Whatever it was, kid picked a poor moment. To no longer take being put through the wringer. To point his finger... "You don't have the first clue..."

Ooh Kamara could take that pointing finger and shove it somewhere... Boy and his gone-sideways hair... But... Were they getting somewhere? She pressed... She dared...

"Then *give me* one..."

"What for! You're the one going off to grad school! You're the one leaving–" TJ's pointing. TJ's clap back. Ran right into a–

SLAP!

Cuz Kamara wasn't havin that. The blaming. The shaming. She'd been there. *So goddamnit TJ don't you dare! And omg. Did she just go there? Revive her father's curse? Only... worse! She didn't lay it on a cheek below the waist. She'd smacked the boy... right in his face!*

Kamara... had to leave the place...

Oh but lucky T...

At the door was G. "If you slapped her like that, you'd be in jail. But you know, guys and girls are the same." G leaned his head into the hall. "Except when it's not convenient to be!"

"Jesus Christ, G!" began T. "Shut the FUCK up!"

TJ took a step to climb his ladder. But between the shots–the ones earlier that day and the one right then–

T lost his balance. Fell back.

Kid passed out. Right on his back.

Kamara stormed out the DOG house front doors. *Ooh men! To hell with all of them!* Dog House, ha! They were pigs in a pen! Dumb in high school and now dumber even! Their sole mission to spread semen! Buncha fake He-Men. Buncha heavenless heathens! *Ugh now she's quoting a rhyme T penned!* Stomping so mad she could scream and... Eat some... Cold Stone ice cream and... Their nights. Their walks. Their talks. Other times... The weight on his face. His gaze into space. *Something* locked in his safe... *Ooh feelings get out of the way! She just wanted to hate!* But that one feeling... she just couldn't shake. That maybe... they could be great...

Kamara looked back at the DOG house. Disappearing behind the hill... *Nah that feeling was fake. It was too late...*

Kamara beat feet. Past the "man"made lake.

Then hours later. Kamara still awake.

Lying on her couch alone. Soaking in that sad tone.

147

Wondering if the music-loving boy. Ever heard.
"If I Were a Boy."

TRACK 15. TERRIBLE TONY

FRANCO DROVE OUT TO AMBOY. As usual after wrapping on the mats. It kept his habit under wraps. As did his daily stop at the hardware store. Snag supplies for the next repair on his list. Then slip next door to the liquor store. To get his fix. Keep the demon at bay. Make the next day. Just a single 24-ounce can. Franco even switched to the lightest beer of the big three. Ninety-six calories times two. A daily sin if he was tryin to sink to 170. But to throw at 185? He needed some size.

It's one thing to eat healthy to maintain or lose weight. But to eat healthy *and* gain weight? While burning thousands of calories everyday? Franco had to eat all day. Before the final weight cut, it was safe to swell all the way to 200. And Joey had him lookin like a Spartan—*300*. Put Franco through one of them months that turned a muscled man into a monster. The pigeon-toed wrestling side walks down the sidewalk. *With 225 pounds on his back.* Franco's gluteus maximus stretched to the maximus. As Franco joked like Maximus... *Are you not entertained!* As Joey held his thumb sideways like Joaquin Phoenix. As Franco's quads burned hotter than Phoenix. As the old fighter rose like a phoenix. Back from his seven-year exodus. Like he was Moses in *Exodus*. A complete makeover from the Moses movie Franco grew up with. As he got a muscle makeover from the kid he grew up with. Bench press. Power cleans. Squats while Joe would implore Franco: *Ass to grass, let's go!* Then calling Franco, *Skipper. Ya know, one of them big upper body guys that skips leg days.* When Joey knew damn well Franco never skipped legs. But at some point, your legs were your fuckin legs. And all that back-breakin lifting with all Joey's ball-breakin comments... was *after* sprinting the high school track. With a parachute on Frank's back. *Against the wind.* As Joey sung, "Against the Wind." And all *that* was after swimming laps at The Racquet Club. *The butterfly stroke.* Franco dolphin kicking like he was Rob Schneider in *The Animal.* But Franco had to admit. Joey had him feelin like an animal...

Franco's metabolic furnace torched all the food that came his way. Like he was a hulking horse on unlimited hay. The breakfast mountains of nuts, seeds, and grains. Franco chompin like a rat gone insane. Then eatin eggs till he wanted to puke. Like he was Cool Hand Luke. Or Joey Chestnut with a full gut. Yet Yo still made him bury pounds of berries. Shit, Franco coulda went through lunch without a single munch. Instead he was goin cuckoo over the pound of cous cous. Eatin too much tuna like he was Nick Kroll. Slamming sushi roll after roll. Chomping baby carrots. *While Basayev wore karats. The belt.* Franco meanwhile belting spoonfuls of quinoa even thougha he don't knowa how to pronounce it! And dinner? He denounced it! Sackin sacks of potatoes. Crushing kale. Barehanding whole chickens like it was Medieval Times. Weekends slamming Julie's salmon wrapped in spinach and soaked in olive oil. Like he was Popeye and she was Olive Oil. Not to mention the never-ending snack breaks of bars, smoothies, avocados, broccoli, bananas. Franco was goin bananas! But the saving grace... *He wasn't even close to overweight.* It didn't matter what else he ate! Joey even told him, *Sure, top it all off with ice cream, pizza, n pasta. Eat at Red Lobster like a blazed Rasta!* But nah. The fighter passed on all that. Saved it all for the nightcap. The capstone on the 24-7 drilling, cross training, sparring, healthy eating, film studying, unwinding, and sleeping. The nightly capstone that helped Franco sleep better. Embrace the next day like when Cobain hugged Vedder. Hell, even the undefeated Floyd Mayweather had a high-sugar habit. And Franco could still cut to 185 with a shit. So yeah, he had his one drink every night. *No one could tell him shit.*

Now it was the week before the fight. And yeah, he had to keep his moves tight. Impress the press. This go-around, Franco sittin at the dais as stacked as a Roman soldier. The training camp war before the war over. But the training-shortened days. Gave way. To longer nights. To an even bigger fight...

Week one of Project Restore The Project was cleanup and kitchen stocking. Along with mattress delivery n coppin a couple chairs from the curb. Talk about ghetto. Franco stole garbage from the ghetto! The second week was window repair and lighting. The third was carpeting and related carpentry. In the fourth, spackle was tackled. Followed by the fifth for painting. But the sixth. The sixth was still waiting...

A final battle General Franco readied for. Returning from Amboy with extra supplies. Riding shotgun in a big brown bag the size of Macy's Big Brown Bag.

Franco's car radio played "Manic Monday." An oldie but goodie. And when did it become an oldie? Franco remembered when it was a newie. He was 11 and it was around 11. The delightful song was on Z100. On Little Franco's alarm clock radio in his room. Until his old man raided the room. Yanked it out the wall. *Fuckin kid, 11:00 pm, what are you thinkin! This noise is gonna drive me to drinkin!*

Franco hurried across the project parking lot. The brown bag crumbled under his arm like an underinflated football.

He touched down inside his apartment. Did what he always did from there. Made his dinner. Ate. Readied to fix up something...

Only it was the sixth week and the place was at its peak. The white walls as fresh as Impala white walls. And the downstairs rooms' lighting was three-for-three. Franco admired them with "okay" symbols over his eyes–like he'd dropped a three.

So Franco moved on to his bonsai tree. Bestowed by Brazil and the team. On the last of three-a-days. A gift that was both honorable and honored the old-timers' roots. With all of their joking that Brazil was Miyagi and Franco was Daniel-son. Brazil's passing off of Franco to one of his students in the also-ran annex. Proved to be the key to connecting Franco's mind and body. And to disconnecting from Brazil's holds...

Just a month ago, the task of escaping Brazil's best mount was insurmountable...

Franco's back fastened to the mat. Brazil's wrecking-ball ass wrecking any attempts to bridge. His knees nestled into Franco's armpits like Ray and Stevie to two pianos. Playing notes on Franco's lymph nodes. Brazil's flippers shooing foot traps–the Jiu-Jitsu master turned "Pinball Wizard." All the while, his weight crushing Franco's thorax. Like Brazil was modern society. Franco the Lorax.

But this past Friday, Franco's hips were more flexible. His

present mind more mendable. As he pulled a move commendable. After all the bridge closings. After all the foot trap fails. After the shrimp couldn't even manage a shrimp roll. The shrimp–check that, *former champ*–made two C-clamps. Daggered his curved hands into Brazil's pits. Rocked the rock for all of eight milliseconds. Eight milliseconds that allowed Franco to swing his *feet* up to Brazil's pits. Replacements as sure as Keanu in *The Replacements*. Franco's freed-up hands meanwhile bench pressed Brazil like he was that three-plate bar Yo'd been loading lately. Only Franco heaved this load past his head. Then rolled back on his Nina-stretched back–

Brazil face-down on the mat–

Franco in an ankle attack–

As Ray and Taz clapped that!

And with that. The three-a-days were a wrap. Topped off with Franco's Woodbridge-grown garden handing a plant to their champ.

The bonsai tree that Franco was now tending to. On the last Monday night before the fight. A little water. A couple clips. Then. Franco watching the kitchen clock tick. Fuck. *It was only six.* Franco thought about calling Joey. But he had a shift. Driving Uber n Lyft.

The dining table's brown bag begging to be opened...

Franco had half a mind to breeze out to Branchton for the night. But the Jersey rush hour was worse than the third *Rush Hour.* And Brazil was of course busy with either the business or the brood. Taz too. Tangled up with his tots or his Thai joint. The Monday Nelsons busy puttin the world in full nelsons. Nina spending her Monday nights at the b-ball courts. Franco the ex-baller had half a mind to join her. Like they were Al and Jackie Joyner. But the fighter couldn't risk. An ankle twist...

Franco sighed. Sat at the old olive table. With the brown bag. Starting at it. As the clock ticked.

The moment so quiet... Franco could hear his heart. Tellin him... *He and T had grown apart.* Franco still watched *Sanford & Son.* The kid liked Mumford & Son. Or was it Sons? Franco's mind was in anarchy. Like clips of *Sons of Anarchy.* The show's creator from next door in Rahway. At least that's what T say. Franco was still stuck on Tony Soprano. Still believin...

Franco pounded the table– *He was fuckin leavin...*

He left the brown bag all alone...

Headed upstairs all alone...

His only plan was to turn in early, his last resort. Like when he couldn't afford a nice restaurant and went to Dick's Last Resort. Feeling right then like he was wearing one of them silly hats the restaurant puts on ya. When the waiter curses you out and serves you lasagna.

Franco lay in bed at 6:15. Chalked it up as a meditation session. Ran through each and every lesson. Even ran back all the Basayev film sessions...

Hours down.

But hours to go...

Franco recalled fights by his favorites. T-Wood. With a swag like he's from The Wood. Ronda. Human anaconda. The man named Silva. With the game of gold. Edgar. "The Answer." To impossible questions. Cowboy. What a kicker. Puntin dudes like a Cowboys kicker. And Holly. On some "Larry the Hitman" Holm. And ooh, Dominick Cruz. Kid with all the right moves. Like he's Tom Cruise. In *All The Right Moves.* Then that last fighter. That Franco saw and saw and saw. *Dillashaw.* The five-seven phenom. With that first name. T. J.

Franco turned on his side. Faced away from his door. As

he did since four. Away from his old man. Toward the world. The world surely better. Back then anyway. But why now? Franco's old man was gone. And the fuckin world... Franco's mind whirled... *On the surface, he had nothin to complain about. So why inside, there was nothin but pain about?*

Franco tried to shut it out as he shut his eyes. Tried to forget about his downstairs prize...

But he heard someone of size...

Someone so big, the carpeted stairs still creaked...

As did the bedroom door's hinges...

As the demon croaked, "Who the fuck are you kiddin?"

Franco turned slower than a hot dog on the rack at 7-Eleven. "Gotta get up early is all."

"Bullshit," bellowed the demon at the door. "You got two minutes. To get your ass the fuck downstairs."

Franco buried his head under his pillow...

Only for his *own voice* to say hello...

Ayy Francooo the Herooo. Right, Basayev's the bad guy. Well which one? Has been in the cage gettin it done? Which one? Is on Insta with his son? So when the fuck are you gonna come correct? How's T—have you even checked? Oh yeah you're a real character with your Jersey how you doin? But like, how's he really doin? You KNOW he's been stewin. But you act like you ain't clued in. Oh now you're shakin... Where's the gin? That's why you really agreed to this apartment ain't it? Up Woodbridge's anus. Cuz your ass belongs here! Now go downstairs and drink some beers! Come on, let's get goin on the real plan. To fuck off and become your old man. You fake motherfucker. When you gonna wake motherfucker? To the earthquake motherfucker! One that blows away the Richter. You fake-ass Mike Richter. That save. When the Rangers rallied and won the Cup. So come on Franco, what's up? You their all-star defenseman Brian Leetch? Or. Are you just a fuckin leech?

"Get the fuck down here!" The demon's voice boomed through the room.

Franco rose from bed. Began the walk. Hearing Of Monsters and Men. "Little Talks." Cuz the monster and man. Were gonna have a little talk...

Franco staggered down the stairs.

Approached the figure. Now illuminated by the dining area light... *Franco wished it was The Frog. Wished it was the ghost of his old man. Wished it was some cruel joke played by Joey...*

But no. It was Terrible fuckin Tony.

Soprano wasn't the only Tony in Jersey with a bad half. And so twisted was Franco's, he started to laugh. His jovial genie out of the bottle. With his triple chin and nose of gin. Looking just like... *him.* Franco. Just... Bigger. Fatter. Paler. Yet with darker eyes. Long lashes givin him an extra singe. *A Clockwork Orange.* His long hair meanwhile unkempt and uncut...

"You even got me a chair!" The deformed dopple's voice deeper, hoarser, harsher than Franco's. Even in laughter.

Franco crooked his head. Why the fuck did he get *two* chairs? Franco's shoulders dropped as the answer dropped into his lap. *So he could drink with this guy.* Franco could read that Tony was ready to get blitzed easier than Tom Brady reading a blitz. So Franco did the same thing Tom Terrific would do... He audibled.

Broke for the kitchen–

"Gotta grab my phone and keys–"

"Have a fuckin drink with me–"

Terrible Tony rose. Looked down from his gin nose. The bear pawed Franco back into his chair. Held a long look with those long lashes...

As Franco looked over to his keys and phone on the counter– "It's just uh–"

"Uh duh yeah blah blah blah," blabbed Tony as he settled back into his seat. "Put those fuckin hands to use and crack us some fuckin beers." Tony's fists to the table driving his point home.

Franco tried to keep his hand steady... Pulled a 30-pack from the overinflated football. The Tom Brady fan working on his own Deflategate. Fuckin Franco and his two sides. Giants fan *and* Tom Brady fan. *Find your fuckin footing man!*

"Fuckin warm," croaked Terrible Tony.

"Fridge is full."

"Oh yeah. All that hoity toity horseshit you been eatin. What are ya gonna die? From some cheese fries?" Tony gnawed as he pawed at Franco. "What's that saying Mr. Nelly, Mr. Dead, once said? *'You're like the five people you hang out with the most.'* [16] Well. You've become a real fuckin joke. As square as this table!" Terrible Tony pounded it. "I'm a little sick and tired of you never visitin your old man. All he asked, *all he asked,* as his liver shriveled and his belly ballooned... is that you come to his grave and have a drink with him. And The Frog? He's no good no more either, is he? Where would you be without him? Punk-ass kid back of the restaurant washin dishes spic n span. Then partyin like a Peter Pan. The Frog... *The Frog* made you a man. And Joey. All the trainin and jokin. But where's the drinkin and tokin? Speakin of, what the hell ever happened to that guidette you used to bang?"

Franco made two fists. Grilled the man with two tits...

Rolling out of his wife beater.

Franco ready to throw a heater–

"And ME!" roared Tony. His biggest wrap yet rattling both the table and Franco. "Keepin me locked in the fuckin dungeon. Like I'm Chunk from The Goonies." Tony motioned to the great below. As his other hand tilted his can.

---

[16] Coach Nelson would want to own. That he didn't make that up on his own. Proper credit goes to Jim Rohn.

He motioned for Franco to hand him another...

"Tell ya what I do appreciate, though. All the food you been feedin me. Throwin dishes of denial down the stairs. Sides of self-doubt. Endless pots of self-pity." Tony patted his gargantuan gut. "Not to mention those party trays of inferiority. You could serve a sorority!" Tony pawed his pal. "Oh and how could I forget? The to-go boxes full of regret. And your funny little apértifs of anger..." The amused Tony took a little swig. "As much as I appreciate all that, though..." Tony leaned forward. "I been down there waitin on the main course..."

Franco sat at the old olive table waitin to be served. Like when his hungover old man scrambled to scramble eggs...

"All this anticipation you've built... So where is the fuckin GUILT!"

Franco fought off his startle–

But Tony was just gettin started–

"Lettin your son wilt. Like you don't know he's on tilt. Worse than Phil Hellmuth in '08. You still *pretendin* it's '08..."

"I'm gonna talk to him. Soon as I get past this fight."

"Yeah right. Pass me another Lite." Tony crushed and chucked his current one. "And would it kill ya to buy some Bud Heavy?"

Franco cracked his neck. Cracked another...

"Eh, a beer is a beer is a beer," sighed Tony. "Kinda like how a queer is a queer is a queer."

Franco shot forward–

"What?" shrugged Tony. "Ya know. Like the one... *that raped your son.*"

Franco stood up–

Tony paused mid-sip. Warned from foam lips... *"Watch it..."*

"Don't even know who did it. Long time ago..."

"Oh right your boy's doin much better now. Tell everyone about Wall Street. As your little shirt traps the heat. As your little heart beats. Thinkin of T and his drooped eyes. *Oh yeah, everything's fine...*" Terrible Tony added an A-okay sign.

"Ah he's Julie's boy anyway." Tony toasted and drank away.

"Say what?"

"Little one. Big brain. Just like Julie. *And the exact fuckin opposite of you.*"

Franco gritted his teeth...

As a grin ran across Tony's chin... "Let it go..."

"What..."

"That pussy-ass princess movie you watched with Kyd."

Franco again shifted to the balls of his feet...

As Terrible Tony did him one better. He rose. And sang louder than his old man ever yelled. "*LET HIM GOOO! LET HIM GOOO!*"

And that's when Franco let it go—

He shot up straight— Delivered a straight kick—

—straight to the heavyweight's heart. BOOM!

Courtesy of the people Franco'd been hangin out with lately... *The fight team.*

As Terrible Tony's crash shook the walls...

Franco grabbed his phone.

Had twelve missed calls...

TRACK 16. MIDNIGHT

TJ OPENED HIS EYE. His other stuck to the tile. Fused by the remnants of a spilled gin & tonic.

His open eye tracked an ant in his own little heaven. *Musta been one of those ants from T's pants. That just had to dance.* They musta all got out. They were all over. Made T wish he could do his life all over. Recapture the innocence of those harmless souls. Those harmless souls who'd never chase "hoes." Harmless innocent souls. Who had no idea. T could just get a hose...

But nah no way. They had to stay.

As for TJ...

His eye tracked from the ant pack to his cell. Also on the cold tiles of his cell. Eh–room. That felt like Hell. If only T could dial Heaven. Ask God why was he drivin him psycho.

He did the next best thing. He dialed Franco.

Once every five minutes for an hour. Forget anything else. Even a shower. T's body hit by a storm. Without power. Lying on the tiles next to his bar. Listening to Kendrick Lamar. *Damn TJ was rude. He'd even stolen her dude!*

But it was the next artist on the hits playlist. That drove

the final stake into his heart. Christina Perri. "Jar of Hearts." The cold tune crushing the cold dude. Topless on the floor. *Oh sure! Always hung up on Lenore! What about the hearts you tore! You've carried on like this before!*

Twenty-one and already a bastard. By 31, he'd be a complete fuckin disaster. He'd heard H— S— on the radio. Waxin about the abused. How they were doomed. Then a psych class reading. Heeding the same warning. So T'd promised himself. He'd kill himself before he hurt anyone else...

TJ felt his slapped face. A reminder. He was a little late. Still. *He had to break the curse. Before it only got worse...*

TJ stared down his demon...

Once again waving to T... From a balcony...

T'd jump high on three. Make sure the demon hit the ground first. Go out on watching him burst...

TJ took a final look at his cracked phone. Could barely make out the time. But it was just right. Minutes to midnight.

"Let's go."

It was the first time TJ ever talked out loud to his demon. And it would be his last.

TJ spiraled up the balcony staircase. Rain railing the railings.

T dizzied as he reached the roof. Headed for the back ledge. The one that would give him an edge. The mansion's rear rising from a cliff's edge...

The shirtless, shoeless kid looked below. Between his pale toes...

Down the mammoth mansion...

Down the cliff's face...

To the final resting spot. The riverside rocks.

All in all a fall of eight stories.

To end his life's story.

TJ. Hanging ten on the concrete giant like Laird
Hamilton. Peering at Broadway lit up with *Hamilton*. About all
T could see. Through the rain. Beneath the fog. The show's
fan ready to step over the edge. As his own lines haunted his
head...

Sick as my secret
Just wanna secrete it
Drag it out beat it
But it's undefeated

Stuck a stake in my head
A hole in my soul
A dart in my heart.
I'm a minute from dead
I'm no longer whole
I've fallen apart.

My eyes peeved black-eyed peas
Lips blue as the moon above
T.i.am peacin the pleas
Nowhere is the love.

TJ heard it *over and over*. At least it was about to be. *Game
over*. Soon as T. Counted to three.
One. The wind howled. Like God was an owl. *Fwooooh*...
Two. The rain pelted the paved roof. Pelted T as he bent
his knees... *Fwooooh*...
Thr–

"Laveranues Coles."
That phrase T learned. When Hurricane Sandy hit Jersey.
The insurance clause apparently a clause in his own

163

constitution too...

Franco standing there. At the spiral stairs. Coming with the unexpected quip. Like a hook from the hip. A surprise strike that landed so well, it turned T 180 degrees. As he stood in the rainy 40 degrees...

"What?"

"I say Laveranues Coles, you say..."

That old game they used to play. Cut right to the heart of something in three words or less...

"Explosive receiver."

Franco continued toward T...

"I say Carlos Santana, you say..."

"Musical genius."

"I say RA Dickey, you say..."

"All-time knuckleballer."

"I say Oprah Winfrey, you say..."

"Force of nature..."

The soaked kid's own force of nature helping him down...

Standing with him in the downpour...

As Franco's words outpoured... "I been thinkin. That what happened to you... is botherin you. Like... real bad. Like... it's eatin you alive. Like... you're afraid it might define you."

Rain drops ran down the nodding kid's face...

Dad's too. Hoodie down despite the downpour... "Everybody I just said. Been through somethin like you been through." Franco exhaled Hudson fog. "Now hear how they been defined by you."

TJ's nod shook loose tears...

"And it ain't just famous people. I've lived long enough. Met enough people to know. People you pass every day. From here to Manhattan. Have overcome... all kinds of... drama..."

"Trauma?"

Franco nodded. "Really successful fuckin people. And they call em... survivors? I dunno. To me, they're a lot more than that..." Franco searched for the right word, his right hand rolling...

TJ's mind already scrolling... His street father not even knowin. He was hittin the same themes. As scholar Yvonne Dolan. The societal studies minor now remembering *Beyond Surviving*. The societal studies minor... who was crying.

Franco saw the tears running down the kid's face. Pulled him in for an embrace. Before the behemoths of Manhattan. Besieged by fog. Franco huggin away. Now *his* mind pluggin away...

"Who's the biggest opponent I ever faced?"

"The Prince?"

Franco shook his head.

"Basayev?" returned T between sniffles.

"You gotta understand somethin." Franco broke the embrace. Paced the paved roof...

"Your biggest opponent in life..."

The college honors student hung on his street father's wisdom like he was Einstein unlocking the mystery of the universe...

"Your biggest opponent in life... is YOU."

TJ's forehead wrinkled so hard he'd have to iron it out. But Dad's tone... Tougher now...

"Back in the day, I used to think that you could work toward one thing. World champ, millionaire on Wall Street– whatever. Then it would be all good. Game over." Franco fired a finger– "But it ain't never over!" Franco fired it again. This time to the great beyond– "Life is gonna push you to the ledge. Again. And again. And again." As Franco pointed. Again. And again. And again. "And it's on YOU to push

165

back!"

The kid with goose-bumped ribs nodded. Shivered.

"You have any idea how lucky you are to even be here?" Franco motioned to the world at-large. "And all you got goin for you? Not to mention– *the people you'd hurt–*" Franco bit his hot-tempered tongue–

As TJ buried his face in his hands. *His dumbass three-count. His dumbass assumption that it would only hurt him.* "I didn't even– think about–" The choked-up kid couldn't bring himself to say Kyd. He hadn't seen her in weeks. Mom on Fridays as Brawlers wrapped up its lease...

Franco put a hand on his son's shoulder. "It's alrigh–"

TJ brushed it away– *"It ain't alright."*

Franco took a breath. Soaked in the nearby brownstones. "You're 21 years old." Zeroed in on the rainbow of lights emanating from a three-story house party. "Your head is so far up your ass... it's a miracle you could see at all."

"Is that... an insult or a compliment?"

"I dunno, little of both," huffed Franco. "That's life I guess. Good n bad. Dark n light. All that. Just... gotta keep grabbin for the good half."

The two took a breath. Soaked in Hoboken.

"Ya only live once ya know," added Dad.

Oh did T know. Yolo. But... "What do you mean?"

"I dunno..." Franco searched the city fog like it might spit out the answer... "Make it one you're proud of."

TJ exhaled cold breath like a dragon letting out fire.

Then watched as Dad peered across the way...

"You'll be seeing it real good Saturday," concluded T.

Franco bit his lip. "It's funny. The fight game's taken me all over America. Across the Atlantic even. But I still never been right there." Franco pointed across the Hudson. "Right. There." Then shrugged. "Not that I could see it..."

"There was a house trip to a Knicks game last month."

"You go?" asked Franco as he rocked a Rock eyebrow.

TJ shrugged. "What did you used to call us? When me, you, and Mom used to take the train into Penn Station?"

"We were underground, under the garden. Like the Fraggles," Franco said with a laugh.

"Well if Fraggles aren't welcome up in the garden... Figured we better go in together."

Franco paced...

Even flexed as he looked across the way...

As he heard Kanye n Jay. "Run This Town."

Wonderin... Could he actually take Basayev down?

TJ meanwhile took a last look over that ledge. Felt his hair soaked against his forehead. The kid's bow broken. On the roof in Hoboken. Like Eric's in *The Little Mermaid*. When the seaman. Defeated his demon. Of all movie scenes, that's the one T thought of. As he stared down at those riverside rocks. Under the moon.

Those rocks that were dark.

And glistened of goo.

TRACK 17. HOBOKEN

TJ DROVE AWAY FROM THE DOG HOUSE. Drove
away from Hoboken. Drove deep into Jersey. Dove deep into
his mind. He didn't know if he and Kamara could make up.
But his mind was made up. He was gonna show her who he
was. With no makeup. Show her the last piece of the puzzle.
That had kept her puzzled.

TJ cut across the lawn. Toward the front door of the
house that looked like something out of his suburban sitcom
imagination. The house home to the Francos 2.0. Franco.
Julie. Kyd. And oh yeah. *This kid.* Welcome any time.
Although Mom would probably have his ass if she heard him.
Slippin in at one in the morning without warning...

TJ took his sneaks off. So he could sneak off–
And almost tripped over–
Auggie Doggie. Half-pit bull half-lab. A wild tail wag.
Dark as the night. Whimpering at the sight...

T. Taking a knee.
Petting Auggie.
Auggie who followed as...
T cut through the living room of the modern Franco

family. Like he was a cast member of *Modern Family*.

Then up the stairs. Damn, they were made out of good wood. Not like their old house in The Wood. Creaks for weeks.

TJ made it to the bedroom he called home for his final three years of high school. The one he didn't bump his head on when he woke up. The ceilings eight-feet tall all around. In the house with central air. Oh how Little T used to vent. About their old house's no-AC vents.

The come-back kid looked to his old desk of mahogany. Where he used to sit like a captain of industry. Cranking out essays steada hangin with eses. Its brass handles now glistening in the darkness. But for all the positive thoughts that danced through T's head...

There was still the monster under his bed.

TJ took a breath. Got down on all fours in the dark room. Darker yet what loomed. Like a poisonous shroom...

TJ plucked it from deep within the darkness...

The rolled-up front page of the *West Jersey Journal*.

TJ unraveled the story.

That had unraveled his life...

YOUTH ATTACKED IN SEXUAL ASSAULT

TJ stared. And stared. And stared. At that headline.

Then dead into the eyes of the artist's sketch. Fucking at-large guy looking so sketch...

TJ's eyes then trailed... Down to the details...

His mind sailing away... Recalling it like yesterday...

When the undersized soph was walking home from wrestling tryouts. The weight-cut waif taking the tracks because the rural sidewalks (or lack thereof) were flooded. Then from the tracks to a path through the woods. When a "man" jumped out– The vagrant's flannel worn out–

T's heart stopped–

Oh. He was an undercover cop. Saying... *One false move and T would be shot?*

He dropped the badge. Handcuffed the kid for trespassing...

The kid... *suddenly feeling his whole life passing...*

And was the badge before his feet... *plastic?*

That's when he did something drastic...

TJ ran. Screamed. *"HELLLP!"* In a singular guttural way. Never before or since that day. *"HELLLP!"*

Over and over as he ran the wooded track...

Hands cuffed behind his back...

"HELL–" The last thing T yelled...

When he was sacked. Shoulder separated on impact.

The "man" on his back. Saying the trespassing punk would have to pay a price. *And boy would it feel nice...*

Fucker clawing his hair–

TJ gasping for air–

Between face mashes into the mud–

Some time later. His pants back up.

Released like a pout-pout fish. Blub. Blub. Blub.

Twenty-one-year-old T caught his breath. Thought reading the details would make him fume. But staring them down... it's like his heart... had found room. To accept this part of him. To vow that it would drag him down no longer. In fact... *It would make him stronger.*

TJ rolled out with the rolled-up paper hearing "Stronger." And what was really cray... It wasn't Kanye's. It was the one by the artist on little sis's door. TJ thinkin, *Damn son! Inspired by Kelly Clarkson!*

TJ threw a peace sign over his heart. To the girl on the door and the one behind. Ready to leave his past behind.

Scratch that–carry it with him. Share it with the girl he was missing...

TJ descended from the second floor...

Put on his sneaks at the front door...

"Franco?" Mom approached in a string-less old Woodbridge hoodie...

"Franco Junior," whispered T.

"What are you doing–" Julie saw the newspaper. THE newspaper... "Are you okay..."

TJ looked at the paper. Looked at Mom. The concern on her face revving from two to three to four...

T remembering when her jaw hit the floor. Seeing the 15-year-old at the front door. The handcuffed kid who had to knock with his head. His face bloody and muddy. Saying he was attacked by somebody. Yeah buddy. A not-so-good day. From the good old days.

But now TJ... *felt okay*. As his nod conveyed...

"Are you sure?"

"I mean..." TJ nodded to the paper. "I'm on the right track."

"What are you doing with it?"

"I wanna share it with somebody."

Julie gave TJ a crooked look. In the dark, he looked just like Young Franco. Giving her as sure a look as Young Franco did the day she met him. "Must be someone pretty special–" choked Julie.

TJ nodded. And nodded. As the tears streamed. And streamed.

Mom pulled in the kid. Crying on the outside. But inside... *he beamed.* He was a Franco. *The love on that team.*

TJ walked up to Kamara's brownstone. His heart racing over

the impending drop. Like he was Tom Hardy in *The Drop*.

One arm securing a bulging folder.

The other arm swinging at the shoulder. The shoulder dislocated on that dark day. The one that dislocated his Ivy League wrestling future. Dreams of Wall Street recruiters.

So instead...

It was JSUH.

That...

Special place.

Just...

Look at her face.

Kamara had swung the door open. Her hair all out of sorts. Her thighs stretchin her shorts. *Now the boy comes to work it out?? When she's half-dressed for a workout??*

"I just... want you to have somethin. I don't know if you feel like somethin's off about me or somethin..."

"An inability to pronounce the letter 'g'?"

TJ smiled. Handed the newspaper over. "It ain't good... Which reminds me." He pulled a purple notebook from the folder. "I started a new rhyme journal."

"So the not-good article reminds you of your rhymes?"

"I mean... it's something more uplifting. For after you read that depressing-ass article. But who knows. Maybe the rhymes suck too," T conceded with open arms.

As Kamara motioned for the notebook. With open arms...

Kamara played it cool as he walked away. Closed the door. Even slowly locked it. Then charged to her couch. Like she was shocked by a socket.

The newspaper headline delivered another jolt. But her eyes kept reading. Despite a mind in revolt. The details were

173

terrifying. Horrific. Kamara's eyes rushed through the story so grim. And to think... *The boy was him.*

The boy who stapled a page to the back of the paper...

Kamara,

To keep it one hundred, I don't know where the effects of this incident end and my own idiocy begins. Maybe I've taken too many of the wrong hip-hop songs to heart. Watch too many antihero shows. Read all the wrong prose. Who knows. Oh and get way too wasted, obvi. Bottom line. The blame is on me.

Lying on your couch. Listening to Jon Stewart talk about morals and values. Morals and values?? I always thought they were for the religious. Or dorks. Who would even write that? A real dork! Anyway. If morals and values are for Jon Stewart. Then they're for this Jersey guy too.

And of all the things from college I value.
Top of the list.
Is you.

Love you all day Kamara Day.

T. J.

The last line imprinted. By a lonely teardrop. As she heard that song her dad used to play. "Lonely Teardrops." Jackie Wilson crooning. Continuing the swooning. Letting her know that T's heart is crying. For a second chance.

And that's when Kamara got up. And started to dance.

Doing that twist. That one her dad taught her. That time he called her. The world's best daughter.

As a second teardrop joined the first...
Kamara opened the notebook.
Read the verse...

"Games"

There's a board game called Life
Another called Trouble
Another called Sorry.
I messed up your life
I'm nothin but trouble
I'm sorry.
You're XBox 360
I'm just an Atari.
A boy n his joystick
Without you I have no joy—
I'm sick.
Navigatin the video game of life
All its devils n demons
My character screamin—
I thought this was supposed to be fun!
Well maybe two players...
Are better than one.

******

P.s. Do you know a good psychologist?

As Kamara smiled...
As her tears dropped...

TJ was on his way to another drop...

He tightened his grip on the steering wheel as he approached the Pulaski Skyway. But. Something was different that day...

TJ cruised over the expanse. Felt like he... *wanted to dance.* And it wasn't the Clonium. He hadn't had one that day. Yet he was... okay. He just kept on along the bridge...

Cruised right into Woodbridge.

TJ parked on Bunns Lane in front of newly-erected apartments. Damn they looked good, no jokin! Projects nicer than Hoboken!

But TJ made his way... to the old end of the block. To the next project on the chopping block.

Franco answered in one knock.

His tank had T shocked– "Damn, you're jacked. You look like... Uncle Joey's been inflatin you with an air pump all month."

"That woulda been a lot easier," quipped Franco. "Anyway, what are ya doin here? I thought it was UPS..."

"Well, I am here to deliver something," T began. "A playlist. For your final run before the fight."

"Where is it?" Franco looked around. Only saw his son's big browns. Sprung to life on that spring day...

"It's online actually."

"Like up in the clouds?" Franco pointed to the sky.

"Something like that. Figured I'd just come by. I can put it on your phone..."

"Come on in. Teach a man to fish..."

"Wow. Place looks good," began T as Franco closed the door behind them.

When Franco did set foot outside for that final run. He saw the note left by his son. Sticking out under Franco's welcome

176

mat. The one with a cat tippin its hat. The one that reminded Franco of Julie reading to their kids.

The fighter reached his iPhone-strapped arm. Picked up the note. Read what T wrote...

Dad,

New day.

New me.

New you.

Let's. Go.

-TJ

Franco started his run. Right along Bunns...
But.
He turned back...
Burned back...
To his apartment.
Came out with keys.
Charged to his Charger.
Down the block it was gunning–
What– *Franco was supposed to be running!*
The HEMI-powered Dodge screamed up the Pike–
Exited–
Flew past the dockworker's old port–
Sped through downtown Newark in Sport–
Franco finally got a hold of the ride. Downshifted to Drive...
Ended it in front of where he last fought. In front of

where he'd left off...

And that's where Franco started running. As stumped as Forrest Gump.

Past the hospital he was born in...

Past the arena he last won in...

And he just... kept runnin...

Franco ran back toward a Turnpike sign. *Had to be out of his mind...* But T's playlist had him choo-chooin with Church. The lover of Springsteen. Hearing "Springsteen."

Franco booted it through the toll booth. *Even took a ticket on his way. Swore he'd pay!* Then navigated across the fork. Chose to head North...

The fighter deked and ducked honking cars.

Then settled onto the shoulder. Relaxed his shoulders. Thanks to T hittin the traveller with "Traveller." This Chris Stapleton guy singin about where he's goin, he don't know. *But he's got to go...*

Franco picked up steam. Like the 80-mile-an-hour trucks whipping dust up. As the track changed. To "Kick the Dust Up." The running fighter laughed. *Listenin to all this country. In the armpit of the country.* Franco would defend Jersey against all comers. But this stretch was rough. Warehouses of rust. Bridges stompin through swamps. Houses overlooking the Turnpike with boarded-up windows. Porches of bored minnows...

"Ay yo! That's Franco!"

Before long, kids were running down the block. Till a fence had them stopped. Their fingers interlocked. Like that time *Franco's fingers* were interlocked in fence. The fresh-faced fighter on the fence... *Trying to find the guts... the rage... to get in that cage...*

"LET'S GO FRANCO!" barked the little boys and girls.

What was Franco just sayin about this stretch of Jersey?

Run it back, scratch it. Forget he ever hatched it. Yeah Franco was backpedalin on his dis. As he backpedaled. And raised a fist.

The kids threw a fit. Let some punches rip. One even yelled, "YOU THE SHIT!"

Yeah Franco was ready to sign the whole area. Give it an extension. As he fuckin flew. Onto the Turnpike Extension. At that fork in the road he usually took the other way. Up to watch the Devils play. But today he had a new hellfire stokin. Blazing a path... *to Hoboken.*

Honking cars started to recognize the man running like he was on fire. Like he was Denzel in *Man on Fire.* As T ran some young buck's "Fire." A song the kids would call... *Fire.*

Man. Nothin like a May day in Jersey. After months of everyone screamin mayday in Jersey. Cold. Snow. Rain. Give Franco sun n some clouds a-gain n a-gain. Ooh and that green over in Laurel Hill Park. Franco wishin Lauryn Hill was parked. The East Orange local with those singular vocals. Wished she was there writin her next record...

As Franco continued the hunt. *For the next win on his record.* Listening to the next record. Trying to right his story. Hearing "Edge of Glory." *God damn Gaga had talent to the max.* And was that... *Clarence...* assassinatin the sax? That's right, it was in fact! Gaga's interview with Stern had covered that fact!

And Franco straight tore the Turnpike apart... When he heard "Tear in My Heart." The song had Franco feeling young and mad in love. When he swore Jewels was sent from above...

Franco's step found yet an extra hop. From Icona Pop. Two girls singin about crashin their car into a bridge? Shit, Franco n Joey once did that in Woodbridge! Franco for once smiling over the duo's crazy young bullshit. As the crazy young duo sung. "I Love It."

And no way Franco was gonna rest as he passed the rest stop. The one dedicated to Alexander Hamilton. As TJ ran "Alexander Hamilton." About a bastard. An orphan. Yeah the Brawler could relate. Sure it was no longer '08. But this song was laying out a new plan... *New York. New Man.*

Franco beat feet toward the Freedom Tower. Damn, did it tower. As T ran "Power." Franco running east and feeling West. Oh and the beeping cars? They were the BEEPing best. Shouting out the fighter from the billboard. Back in '08, The Prince was the pretty one. But this time... The Beast made Franco look good! *Fuckin handsome kid from The Wood.* Yellin back at the cars. *"Ay what's good!"*

Then exited and ran as fast as he could. Onto a Hoboken backstreet. It was fuckin hood. Like Bunns Lane back in The Wood. Franco slapped the sign about baseball n Sinatra *real fuckin good.*

Then ran along warehouses running along tracks. As the playlist changed tracks. To the last of two. *Wait. What did T just do?* This track was the only one to pre-date '08. This track by the original little girl with the voice so grande. Before Gaga. Before Grande. And when the Newark-born boy heard Redman... he straight put it into the red, man. Franco's head no longer murky as he listened to "Dirrty." The song's video was *exactly how he imagined his head.* A rundown warehouse like the ones he ran past. Full of Darkness. Grime. And... Straight-up shenanigans. People wylin the fuck out. Dancin. Partyin. Dressed as furries. The mad fighter now throwin flurries! Like *he* was Christina in that boxing ring. The little knockout. Knockin the big one out. *Like Franco was gonna do to Basayev. No doubt!* And like Redman, the wylin fighter even *started barking.* As he passed wide-eyed yuppies parking. Oh but then there were others. Who slapped Franco five like they were brothers. Shit, he even fist-bumped pre-school mothers!

The sprinting fighter straight-up smokin Hoboken...
A transplant town full of people from all parts.
Like the accented woman that cut straight to his heart—
"You're the reason my girl does martial arts!"
Franco dunno... somethin about it... had him all broken
apart. The accented woman a spark... That helped Franco
break T's final message apart... As he heard the final song
start...

Rhymes from Kendrick Lamar. Giving way to bars. From
music's biggest star...

Franco running swift as he listened to Swift. Remembering
Basayev's thugs. Feeling "Bad Blood."

Franco started mashing lefts and rights. As the last two
songs meshed so right. Artists old and new. Dark n light. East
Coast, West Coast. Man, Woman. *Man, Franco was gonna give
Basayev a whoopin!* Right in front of his provincial pasha saying
the driver of Nelly's "accident" was nowhere to be found.
Buncha fuckin clowns. *Basayev was goin down!*

And that's when Franco saw the sign. Like he was Ace of
Base. And dropped his jaw in awe. Over the place...

The landmark for Sinatra's old apartment. And the memorial
to Old Blue Eyes... had Franco feelin Old Green Eyes. *Nelly.
Gone but not forgotten.* So yeah. Franco wasn't stoppin. *He'd beat
Basayev till they were moppin...*

Franco stamped the sidewalk's Sinatra star with all his
power. *And got star power.* Started running as invincible as
Mario through the square-mile barrio. The force running
through him inside and out... *Nelly power no doubt!*

And Hoboken was dope, no doubt!

Franco blazed down Frank Sinatra Drive. *Man, was it good
to be alive.* Running with a skyscraper backdrop like he was
Little Mac— When he saw—

T! Running like *he* was Little Mac! Even blew right past

Franco–the little kidder! Shouting, "You're all over Twitter!"

Holy shit–all the people with all their phones–running right behind Franco's back! A fuckin wolfpack! Of all ages. Shapes. Shades. Franco could cry–someone throw him some shades!

The old, sweat-soaked fighter tore after the young man– "No fair, you're a fresh man!"

TJ wrinkled his brow over the phrase. Then amped up the race... "Beat you to the dock!"

"Soon, kid..." Junior heard Senior say. "Real soon. But not today..."

The old lion roared as he tore through the concrete jungle. His hind legs motoring. Fronts flailing...

All the way...

To the iron railing.

Senior stepped up for a better look.

Junior joined as...

Franco's neck stretched and stretched and stretched...

The wolfpack packed around. Chattering. Wondering what he had found...

Franco pointed a finger as sure as Brazil's. And said just as ardent. "There it is. There's *The Garden.*"

TRACK 18. THE BOY & THE WOLF

EIGHTY DEGREES AND A BREEZE. Whispering
through the trees. God whispering to T. *An extra nice day this
year. Let's call it forty.*

The sun reflected off his graduation cap. Illuminated his
iris honors chords. As he sat with his cohort. In a campus
quad. Cirrocumulus above. Marking where their limit was.

Parents of business students abound. But T's not around.
The family would be at the next day's all-student graduation.
TJ almost bailed on this business school bally-hoo himself.
But all those classes—he wanted to reward himself.

Apparently by perusing his fixed phone.

At least until the keynote speaker. Moved on from career.
To something deeper...

TJ looked up at the Chief Financial Officer from one of
the chief financial companies on The Street. A glasses-
wearing woman named Amy Pete. Looking like Dr. Goa
from distance. Sustaining a legend's existence...

"'A fight is going on inside me,' an old Cherokee said to
his grandson. 'It is a *terrible* fight. Between two wolves.'"

TJ pocketed his phone...

"One is *Evil.* He is Anger. Ego. Envy. Regret. Greed."

TJ perked up like a wolf in the wild...

"But. The other is *Good.* He is Joy. Humility. Compassion. Generosity. Love."

T almost raised his hand himself–

"'Which one wins?' wondered the boy."

Warm air breezed through the surrounding trees...

As the students hung on the words from Ms. Pete...

"The one that wins. Is the one you feed."

The Cherokee...

The Jersey girl in business attire...

Had T on fire...

"So as you grow in your careers and in life..." continued Ms. Pete. "Do it by feeding the right wolf." She looked to the perked-up pack before her. "For that is how you will truly build personal wealth."

As the grads stood up and clapped...

TJ was on the run as she wrapped!

He dashed across the campus. That four-year experimental canvas. The senior hustling to leave his final mark. *Before it all went dark...*

Finals week had gone by in a flash. TJ had been living with Lance. He forgot all about G. Sori. Old Willy...

TJ cut through a path like a wolf through the woods...

Took out his phone and dialed...

Across campus at the DOG house, a crew rolled out. Brothers wearing collars. Headed for Blue-Collar Scholars. Lance taking the lead for the graduating T.

He and his crew packed into cars to do some good. To help kids from The Wood.

The other crew, though. Walked out with bats in tow.

Young men full of brains and brawn. Young men. Known as
G's pawns. The alpha leading the hungover wolfpack. Bigger
and badder than *The Hangover's* Wolfpack. But nah they
weren't gonna commit any crime... They were just gonna play
the national pastime!

As Lance, Candyman, and co left in cars aligned like an
actual wolfpack...

Dexter and other disciples followed G in a stack...

Across the way... Another mob made its way...

In riot gear. Stomping with dignified paces. As bandanas.
Covered their faces.

A pack with packed pockets. Utility knives, self-defense
Mace, ropes. Nothing silly. Just going to protest. Down at
Old Willy...

Somewhere between the two cohorts...

Kamara was at the food court. Ostensibly to grade
freshman psych papers. But if she was being honest about
what she was doing at that *exact* moment... She was taking a
moment. Inspired to write. But she's not gonna share, alright?
It was embarrassing, okay? Okay okay okay...

Yeah it's the TA
With the T & A—

It's for her alter-ego, okay! Stop! No more-a! It wasn't
even her... It was *Kimura!* It's just... Ruth's show in The City...
She thought she'd write a little ditty. And. Still stuck on the
first hook. Staring at that gifted notebook. *The effort it took!*
And what was the advice that TJ gave? *It's a chance to say...*

whatever's too hard to say. That doesn't make sense! And seriously, he already wrote a whole new song for Ruth's show? But... what if he didn't show? *Have some faith, Kamara! His remorse showed! Watch the boy grow...*

The one calling on the phone...

"Hey–" began Kamara.

"Hey, long story but Sori and her crew are on their way to Old Willy. So is G and some DOG house guys. It's gonna get ugly. Call Sori. Tell her to cut it. Like– right now–"

"Okay..."

"Thanks– Calling G–"

G's unit headed dead for Old Willy. Mummy's undercut flapping in the wind. Baby with a fresh fade for the win. All agreeing... *An attack on Willy's a sin!* So no way would they flounder. *He was their school's founder!*

And that's when G found her...

The sun piercing her nose piercing...

Sori leading her crew toward the statue. Their shell outfits ready to take a shelling. Approaching the bat boys... with their own set of toys...

G could see Sori's auburn eyes...

Ablaze on her shaded face like fire pits in the night. Ablaze with red-hot embers. Because Sori remembers...

It was the first of September. The freshman dressed to impress in her party dress. She even threw on stilettos and straightened her hair. She was gonna be a new woman there! And after the makeup, she had to admit, she was looking bomb. A movie duckling made over for prom! Yes! Her college life would be a rom-com!

Two drinks in, she had not a care. Her hands in the air. Only later was she so appalled. Dancing to "So Appalled." But that night. Her white knight. Had come to life. Like he'd stepped out of her Hollister

*catalog. With his charming dialogue. Forget "Take Me to Church,"
you're my synagogue. As he slid up behind her, her dance pedagogue. A
fucking god. The fact she ever thought that— Oh my god! Must've been
the jungle juice shots. So little. So rocked!*

As for the sex... One of her life's major regrets...

*And it was against her better judgment. Thanks to her impaired
judgment!*

Now look at his tall ass walking her way... *Just like he did
the next day. The dorm hallway. When she tried to chat him up. When
he just said... 'Hey.' Then continued on his way!*

Ooh that freshman September...

DOES HE EVEN FUCKING REMEMBER?

Sori made a beeline for G... *Ooh just looking at him makes me
sick! I'm gonna stab him right in the di—*

Ooh how they *both* descended on the statue. How *both*
their eyes burned like embers...

Because G also remembers...

*Sori and her online stories! How alcohol's a date rape drug. Such a
sly little fox! Blaming it on the alcohol like she's Jamie fucking Foxx!
SHE took those shots. SHE gave consent. So G owes her nothing. Not
even a cent.*

*And yeah, G remembers the next day. What can he say? Did she
have marriage plans? It was a fucking one-night stand! What does she
want to do? Make an earthquake out of every mistake? That's misery
for heaven's sake!*

While G continued straight ahead... the campus was
spinning around... The confused kid wondering... *What was
even happening now?*

*Feels like just yesterday the lanky little guy was in front of the TV
watching that long-legged athlete. The regal man who strolled onto the
talk show before the hooting crowd. The one who said he slept with
20,000... and they cheered so loud. Oh that's the way to be a man...
That's how!*

So... *How come what was true then... wasn't true now? Oh how the pendulum swung, wow. Well. G would balance it. Fucking call him the Tao. Oh right that makes G the bad guy then. While she leads an organization called Move Over Men!*

Now leading her pack like she should be awarded some badge of courage. Ha! She's Henry in *The Red Badge of Courage*. Brewing her man-slamming articles as cruel as *The Crucible*. Whipping up "it's all rape culture" mass hysteria like it's the original Mass hysteria. *Please. You're a joke. You're Belgian Coke. Toyota brakes. Give us all a break. You're not anthrax. You're one of the fakes!*

Sori and G.

Buzzing on that freshman night back then.

Their phones buzzing right then. On vibrate. *Because whoever kept calling. Would have to wait!*

G clenched his Slugger. Yeah he could be a real fugger. But he had his constitution. His lines in the sand. So he turned. *Toward a yes man...*

As G cocked his bat back...

As Sori flashed her blade...

The cops.

Headed their way.

Sirens blaring...

A few holdouts still daring...

To exchange blows.

Until Sori and G gestured no-gos...

The two clans brushed past each other. Carried on.

One group off to play...

"Baseball."

The other off to play...

"Um, paintball. That's all."

"Public property. Get a permit to protest," concluded the coed cops *this close* to making arrests...

TJ watched from the hilltop. Having done what Coach Nelson had done. *Dialed 9-1-1.*

TJ doubled over, *"Fwooooh..."* On one of them weird days when he could see the moon. So, he let out a–

"HOWOOOOO!"

When G made it back to his room–

T was in the middle of another– *"HOWOOOOO!"*

Busy *RIPPING* down a poster. *Schwooot!*

"What the fuck are you doing!"

"I'm a fresh man!"

"You're a senior– You're wearing a fucking– graduation gown!"

"Two words, G! *Fresh. Man.* HOWOOOOO!" TJ ripped down another poster. *Schwoot!*

"Oh and a porn machine? Like we're Charlie Sheen!" TJ ripped the monitor from the desk.

"No, seriously, what are you doing–"

"Winning!" exclaimed T on the balcony. As the monitor took that leap he never took...

"HOWOOOOO!"

"Dude. I think you should take one of these..." G cracked open the kid's Clonium...

"Oh man. You're right," said T as he reduced the throttle...

Then punted the bottle!

Walked right through the Clonium shower. Headed toward balcony flowers...

Grabbed some inglorious books on his way.

And the kid breaking the habit... just had to run

189

"Breaking the Habit."

"Dude I could get five bucks a pill for these..." said G as he scrambled on all fours. Picked up pills all over the floor...

As TJ whipped an inglorious book off the balcony...

G paused on all fours. "Dude, seriously. Are you okay?"

"Dude, seriously. Never been better. Oh and years ago... I was attacked in the woods by a man. Not that he deserves that title. Anyway. Nothing I can do about it!" concluded T with arms out.

"Jesus Christ, man..." G began with an open hand... "I didn't know that..."

"Well now ya do. *HOWOOOO!*"

TJ tossed another book–

As G took cover behind the bar. *His mixed-up mind...* He had to mix a drink...

A G & T.

Only he...

Only poured the tonic.

Wow was T just honest...

G stormed away from the house.

Once again scowling.

Once again stalking the state U.

But this time...

He headed for the gates.

As his mind raced...

His mother. And. Fucking Sori. Wait. Did he... owe her a sorry? No, she owed him one! In class roasting his ass. And today, with her knife! She was gonna take his life!

The stomping kid made two fists. *God damn was he sick of dealing in relatives. Sick of blaming his hurt on his relatives...*

One fist unfurled. Pulled out his phone...

His second fist unfurled...

The kid's texting as intense as his walk... *As his mind confronted their hook-up in the absolute. He'd had too much Absolut. His next-day coldness was too resolute. He could've been kinder. That was his Truth.*

Not to mention...

They damn near killed each other today!

There had to be another way...

But... what would G say?

And what would... Sori say?

He didn't know. As he typed on his phone...

We should talk. No weapons. No wingmen.

Sori's response after consulting K...

K.

Received by G.

He exhaled outside the campus gates.

The college kid then slowed his pace...

Amid yuppies hustling on the bustling drag.

A couple more blocks...

The kid completely heeled.

At the coffee shop.

On Bloomfield.

Out a brownstone blocks back, four girls walked out like the cast of *Girls*.

Sori peeled off first.

Intensified her hop.

As she approached...

The coffee shop.

Candi beat feet onto the following street. The engineering grad in a cap and gown. Off to ceremonies across town.

Kamara also headed that way. To TJ's. So they could peer edit rhymes. Before show time...

Ruth continued toward Manhattan to ready that show. Walked right past Darrell's brownstone. The one with a "ROOMMATE WANTED" sign up. The expelled student's time up.

The redhead pulled her hood down.

Looked like Florence as she ferried over.

Hearing.

"Dog Days Are Over."

For everything TJ ripped down, there was still the banner. Strung across the historic mansion like rims on a Rolls Royce. *Man would it look good on the front lawn. Next to all those books...*

That's when TJ grinned. Undid two big hooks...

The view on the house now much better...

Those giant steel letters:

DELTA. OMEGA. GAMMA.

TJ leaned on the ledge. Like a captain admiring a boat. *The letters' meaning... Determination. Optimism. Growth.*

Yet. The kid's vantage point was what got him the most. From where he stood, those three letters ran backwards...

TJ could only shake his head. As he leaned on the ledge. At Jersey's northeastern edge.

His head free of menace.

Dreaming of tennis.

TRACK 19. THE GARDEN

THE TRIO REVIEWED THE CONTRACT. The incentive-laden contract. Laid out on the kitchen table like an Indiana Jones map. Only to Franco, more confusing...

"What's the bottom line? Brass tacks."

Franco and Julie looked to...

Lama. The sage with the sage eyes. Her layered hair styled as her digits danced before her face. "If you lose. Payout's still bigger than last time."

"So are the cuts to my team," countered Franco.

"Endorsements will be an issue..."

"Back to bein a one-hit wonder."

"If you win..." Lama flipped through the contract, flippant. "You write your own contracts. For your own company. Your own *brand.*"

"What like I'm Wheaties?"

"Something like that," summarized the sage.

"You said you wanted to become a personality," began Julie. Then off Franco's look— *"Whenever* fighting ends."

Lama cut in— "You win? Your next fight. Your next endorsement. Will cover this house. In cash." Lama motioned to the open-air first floor. "My condo could fit in your kitchen by the way."

"Welcome to West Jersey," said Franco with an arm around Julie.

"Your daughter has a frickin forest." Lama motioned past the plate glass...

To Kyd running in the grass. Chasing Auggie Doggie.

"So that's it, I guess." Franco put his elbows on the table. "Either we keep the woods. Or we move back to The Wood."

Franco may have sent Lama out on a laugh, but his head was still doing the math. Calculating... that he hated calculating. He'd had a real job once. Down the docks. The fight game was supposed to be about more than money. But the cold, hard truth. Was that he needed cold, hard cash. A win n he'd even be able to help Joey's ass. His idea for a virtual training venture online. If Franco was the champ of two weight classes? *People all over the world would buy their classes.* Franco a hall of famer in an international sport growing in leaps and bounds. *He'd capitalize this go-around.* But. What if he went down? A loss and Franco would be cashin in the last of his stocks. Shit, he'd be *beggin* to get back on the docks–

Franco stood up. His system shocked–

The feeling clocked. By Julie–

"We can always downsize. I can go back to Jersey Power..."

Franco looked down at his Jewels. *So petite yet so much power...* But the ex-energy company rep had weathered too many April showers. Franco... *Franco* was gonna bring home the May flowers... "I got us. Win or lose." Franco tried to get a read on her blues... "I mean, unless you actually *wanted* to work–"

"I want you," Julie embraced her husband, "to focus on your fight."

Franco & Julie held each other in their spacious home.

But the kid in from outside...

Had them outside...

"Mommy and Daddy sittin in a *tree,*" sung the kid in speech therapy.

Franco sat on the NJ Transit train. In two seats facing each other like loveseats. Only smaller, cheaper, bumpier. But the train's in-motion sounds... the view of his stomping grounds... was just what Franco needed to help him calm down.

The team meanwhile spread throughout the caboose. Giving their fighter room to stay loose.

Until–

"Franco. You got a hot minute?" The big kid's head bobbed by the boxcar ceiling.

"TJ's show? You goin with the old crew? You can duck out early–"

"Thanks. But..."

Franco and his asinine assumptions. He slid his ass over. Ray wanted to talk about somethin...

Ray folded in. Sat across from Franco in seats for guys half their size. All tight like they were about to do a *60 Minutes* interview. "I realized recently–hashtag mindfulness–" Ray nodded over to Nina. Half to lighten things up. Half cuz the kid was gettin all choked up... "I never thanked you. For everything..." The kid from the trailer homes trailed off...

"Nah kid. Thank you. You kept me goin." Franco patted Ray's knotted knee. "I'm sure it wasn't easy goin from starrin to sparrin."

"I underestimated Aram." Ray shook his head. "I shoulda known better. Last time I did that, I got my lip split."

"From when you eked out that first win?"

"Nah, from when I fought your son!"

Franco and Ray burst with laughter.

As Ray rubbed that ole lip.

Then looked to Franco with puppy dog eyes... "What do you think... Nelly would say?"

Just like that. Franco was back. To the night Nelly–*Nelly who helped kid after kid get their asses in gear over all his years*–didn't have much to say about Ray. Nelly who had always had Franco's back. So now. It was time to give back. "He'd say, 'You're doin a heck of a job, kid. Keep it up.'"

Ray nodded. Stood up. Put his fist out for a bump...

"Let's get it."

Franco met it.

The train entered the tunnel... Started to rock...

As it headed under The Garden. On some *Fraggle Rock*.

Franco looked to Brazil. To Joey. To Taz. Then...

To Nina. The young lady always pushin him to nirvana. Like Jay elevated by Rihanna. In that song elevated by her sound. That song that once again made its way around...

As the train let out those creaking-into-the-city sounds...

Franco hearing. "Run This Town."

The fab five escalated out of Penn Station.

Stood before The Garden.

In the New York City night...

Ready to run that town tonight.

In the locker room, Franco wore his old red, white, and blue MMA trunks. The short shorts that had *his legs* looking like tree trunks.

"You look good," said Julie.

"I can see your nipples," needled Kyd.

Julie put the old Woodbridge hoodie on the smiling fighter...

Franco so jacked... *it had never been tighter.*

Then to T– "Ay. Sorry I can't make your show tonight."

TJ smiled over the acknowledgment. "I'm barely gonna make it on time myself."

"Two Francos. Two shows. That's pretty cool."

"Little smaller venue for me."

"So were my first shows."

TJ nodded. "Speaking of shows. This is my first one at The Garden. Make it a good one, alright?"

"Same for you," called Ray as he roved over.

"Dragon put the word out?" figured T.

"You know the crew from The Wood is gonna see what's good. How was that? Was my rhyme good?"

"The fuckin best. Like a Patagonia vest."

TJ and Ray handshake-hugged. Put it all to rest.

But there was new drama... From the new kid...

"TJ said F-U-C-K!"

Julie turned from daughter to son...

"Sorry," shrugged T.

Brazil whistled out the side of his mouth...

Franco's gloved hand pulled TJ in for another handshake-hug.

He kissed Julie.

Shared winks with Kyd.

Then walked over. Joined hands with Joey and Nina. Nina's other tangled with Taz.

The circle filled by Brazil. Brazil who was still moved by Franco making him head trainer. The black man who'd met

197

skeptics every inch of... as Franco put it... this fight called Life. From lenders to vendors. Building his academy one leery learner at a time. But right then. Brazil didn't let any of that show. Didn't trouble Franco. With demons of his own. "Lord. Let Franco know. That he is never alone. We walk with him. We share his mission. So please, Lord, give us the clarity. The vision. To take this decision."

"Amen," wrapped Franco.

Franco then rapped his head. Tried to retain that tidbit. About the Lord keepin his vision dialed...

As he ran out.

To "No Church in the Wild."

As...

The Garden crowd went wild.

For the fighter charging out of the tunnel like the song's featured artist coming out of the closet. Yeah Franco was throwin hooks. As Frank O sang the hook. About a wild with mobs, kings, gods. You alone against all odds.

And when Jay spit about blood on the Colosseum doors...

The fighter straight put the pedal to the floor.

His feet thumpin to the bass bump...

Franco. Running through The Garden. Listening. *To one of the kings of The Garden.* Rappin about dealing drugs, praying thugs, Socrates, Plato. Meshin em all together like Play-Doh. Even sprinklin in some Yeezus n Jesus. *And it all made sense, Jesus!*

Franco stopped aside the cage. Peeled his hoodie off.

The old fighter spread his arms for the final inspection.

Then continued the resurrection...

Over the fence. Like when he was a kid running through ghetto gardens. Only. It was *The Garden.*

Franco stood in the middle of the cage in the middle of the mecca of so many events he never saw. And. He'd love to tell ya he was in awe. But as he looked around the plastic-and-cement bowl... Truth be told... *It was kinda old!*

Kinda like... *him!* Franco realized in the center of the arena so dim-lit. Man, he could be a dimwit. Selling *The Garden* out. As he stood before the sellout...

The crowd that grew so loud...

Fran-co! Fran-co! Fran-co!

The love...

And up above...

That championship banner. *Those '94 Rangers...*

Franco finished soaking in the place. The one just like his hoodie. The Garden. *An oldie but goodie.*

For the champ's camp, though...

They put on a light show. The champ fully cleared by WADA. So Franco had no excuses. Nada. As he watched the volcanic crusher wearing a robe of lava. Along with men in likewise robes as the lights strobed. Surrounding their champ as big as a monster. As his music blared... "Monster."

Ay now wasn't that cray? Basayev was also a fan of Kanye n Jay. *And what did that say?* wondered Franco as Basayev loomed bigger with every step. As the song's hatred grew worse with every verse.

Franco shook it off. Literally. Hopping in his corner as the spotlight illuminated his gray temples. Watching as Basayev thundered into their temple. The re-fed fighter into the 200s. Franco still stuck in the 180s. Like a glam-rocker still stuck in the '80s. Shit, Basayev was *re-re-fed.* Lookin like one of them world's strongest men. The ones with the barrel bellies. Franco meanwhile built like a bodybuilder. Yeah it looked good if you were sellin t-shirts down the shore. But why don't the world's strongest men look like that? *Cuz a chain is only as strong as its weakest link...* Francooo. Hoppin on those little *ankols.* Lookin at his average wrists...

Basayev's meanwhile... *thick.*

Franco didn't let his concerns show as he looked dead into Basayev's dead eyes. Those shark eyes of gray. *That had nothing to say...* thought Franco lost in a moment of reflection. As he looked into his opponent's eyes... *And saw his own reflection.*

The ref broke away.

The fight underway.

The middleweights moseyed around the mat.

And it was Franco who went on the attack. Landed a jab here. Scored a calf kick there. But Basayev was *everywhere.* Bigger *and* faster than the last time they hooked up. Basayev was 25 back then wasn't he? A kid! Well. Now he was all *growns-up* like Mikey at the end of *Swingers.* And a fuckin swinger. Fast. Forceful. Yet dancin around with the grace of Grace Kelly. A linebacker-ballerina. Butkus-Baryshnikov. Hell, that wasn't far off. Basayev *had* been doing ballet. For years. Until the story made the MMA outlets. Until his provincial pasha pulled the plug. And re-trained his thug. *To slug.* But old habits die hard. Like remakes of *Die Hard.* The ballet footwork Basayev had put in remained evident. *And* he could hit–gave Franco the evidence. A slug to the mug. Just a jab–but it *dug.* Rocked Franco's head like a Fraggle. Franco's edge in the round so fragile...

So Franco backed off. Till the sting cooled off.

Rode Brazil's game plan...

Outquick. Outstick...

Gave Basayev fits...

Round two and Franco was still on top. Basayev's pasha about to blow his top. In the front row with one of them hats the shape of a cylinder. As he watched Franco. Fire on all cylinders. The dictator with frustrated reactions. As Franco dictated the action...

He stuck and moved clockwise.

Then countered counterclockwise.

Franco's strikes precise as Basayev was unwinding. Like a broken watch that Franco was winding.

Franco was even able to stop the grappler's shots. His pumped-up legs with extra hops. Allowing Franco to pop in then pop out. Back and forth in a flash like the Roadrunner. He even landed a stunner– A cross after crossing up his stance–

But wow...

Basayev shook it off like a champ.

A champ who got busy in a hurry with a return flurry...

Franco gettin buried...

"This is exactly what Franco wanted to avoid!" Benny "The Force" reinforced. Sitting cageside with co-contributor Karl Blount...

"Any man with any sense wanna avoid THAT."

A slugfest. Basayev at his best...

Franco's head spinning right round like Flo Rida in "Right Round."

Franco now losing the tight round...

Basayev staying right on Franco in the tangle. Taking away any angle...

Franco's face mangled...

And what really had the round two survivor damned...

"Broke my fuckin hand–" Franco whisper-wheezed through his mouthpiece. "Side of his head– Brick wall–"

Brazil clocked the cameras craning in. Clocked his clocked man. "Which?"

The sitting fighter gave the slightest of nods to his right hand.

"We go southpaw. Save the power punches for the left. We up the kicks. And man... *Stay outta the shit!*" Brazil's shorthand for not mucking it up with Umar.

Franco nodded. Hobbled out to round three like an injured lineman insisting he's fine.

Franco was able to knead Basayev with a knee to his barrel belly. And relative to the rest of him... *it was kinda like jelly...*

But Basayev bounced back. Tangled Franco like Nelly...

Franco's fuckin hand. His takedown defense suddenly weakened. He was gonna be sulkin all weekend. The one-handed man down on the canvas. As helpless as a defender down in the post with Karl Malone. Gettin tattooed in the face like Post Malone.

Thanks to Brazil, Franco was able to keep the mountain out of full mount. But the champ clamped. On that old *ankol* of Franco's. The one broken in his last go...

And Basayev wasn't letting go. Twisting with more torque than Franco ever imagined. As Franco rolled with it as best as he could. Thanks to that *other* work in The Wood...

In the annex. *Garbhasana. Ustrasana. Dhanurasana.* Franco twisting more than those tongue-twisting words. Morning after morning. Till he could reach backward and go... *all the way to his toes.* The man with the crab claw arms! *His fight team had him loaded with arms—*

The martial artist spun his body on the canvas. Three-sixty *in the direction of* Basayev's twist. A move that loosened the grip...

Franco scrambled to the canvas. Put up his fists.

The crowd rose with fists of their own—

Brazil's brood in the front row—

"Mr. Francooo!" "Let's gooo!"

But as round three wound down...

Basayev resumed the pound. Wore the one-handed old man down. Then once again took him down...

Fans shared looks all-around...

Like the front row Nelsons. Watching Franco in a half nelson. Watching Basayev's free hand... pummel the man...

Outquick. Doesn't work when you lose your quickness. The old man in there huffing. Taking a stuffing...

Outstick. Doesn't work when you're stuck with a broken hand. Franco a half-nelsoned man. Struggling to rise, to stand...

Basayev smelling blood...

Franco's eyes in a flood. Of blood. Of water. Could barely make out his daughter... *And why'd he even invite her? Fuckin Franco. He dunno. Somethin about how he wanted her to see him in one of his last, if not his last, fights. Before he was one of them old dads at high school graduation. Hobblin to hug his daughter. Them old dads... that suddenly looked like George Clooney compared to him! Shiiiiit,* thought Franco like he was that cop in *25th Hour.*

As Basayev peppered him like Barry Pepper. Coloring Franco's face worse than that time Kyd caked it in makeup.

"I'd say referee Stan Hope should call it. But we've seen Franco like this before. Looks like he'll make round four..."

"Franco. Will see the floor. In round four," concluded Karl.

The one-handed man with the flooded eyes searched for his corner through the mist. *And there were still two more rounds after this?*

If Franco could make it. The man stripped of his tools. Naked. Wandering through The Garden. Having taken a beatin in Eden.

And as Franco fell into his corner at the bell...

He had no idea.

He was headed to Hell.

TRACK 20. THE DEVIL'S DEN

IF HEAVEN IS A PLAYGROUND.

HELL IS A CAGE. Unless you were so insane. You thought it one in the same. To walk in, you had to be part-man, part-monster. Suddenly made sense–Basayev playin "Monster." Yeah Franco loved the cage. When things went his way. But other times. There was Hell to pay. And The Beast was there to collect that day. A messenger who'd bubbled up from that melting pot where Mesopotamia meets Eastern Bloc. No doubt there were people there solid as rock. But this one? This one ran hot. The Devil's dues collector. Billing Franco with shot after shot...

Ayy Francoo. Nice job, buddy. Your half-ass Bible studies. So much for Dante's Inferno. *Shoulda just kept watchin* The Inferno. *And nice work agreeing to the Nina connection. The fuckin mind-body connection. Cuz if ignorance is bliss. What the FUCK is this? All this mindfulness. Awareness. Of the light. AND the dark...*

Franco gettin shelled. Seein Hell. Basayev a stand-in for all nine circles. Franco's blurred vision producing circles. Like The Garden had for the circus. *Shit, this fight was a circus.*

Basayev pummeling. Franco worthless.

Franco thought about thanking God for a minute for his best attribute. His chin. The one he eternally pictures in his first smile at Julie. But right then. That charming chin. Was getting beat to sin. So was it a blessing or curse? That it could take this beating—*an all-time worst.* As blood squirt. Out both Franco's eyes. Franco taking such a yoking... his fuckin nose was broken. As crooked as a corrupt politician. And just as much on the take. Every slug. A fresh pump of blood. More oozing out Franco's mouth. Dribbling down his chin like that time he overfed Baby Kyd.

All on a canvas run red.

The one Franco fell on. Lying there in his own blood. A shell of himself. After a dance with the Devil himself. The one... *inside himself...*

Fuckin Franco. Wallowing over his bad fortune. His broken hand. *Come on Franco! Be a man! What'd you think, this was gonna be easy?* His voice coming through his brain's wires like Yeezy. When he sung "Through the Wire" with his mouth sealed shut. *Yes that really happened! Cuz he would NEVER stop rapping. So get up Franco. Make this happen! Use your God-given legs and your lethal left. And attack this fucker. With EVERYTHING you have left!*

But. Franco's body was frozen. As he lay there eyeing Kyd in a dress from *Frozen.* The little girl rocking over Dad's rocking. The old fighter was ready to close his eyes. To let go. When she started mouthing... "Let it Go." Was it... a nervous tick? Or. Some Young Jedi trick...

Franco's brain whirled like a Dairy Queen blizzard. Back to that frozen night. That blizzard. Last winter. When Julie let Franco know. Brawlers was out of dough. Franco drove through Jersey in the snow. A hell of a day. Especially after the beating from Ray. Franco just wanted to get home.

Shovel their driveway. Have a little booze then snooze. But that Kyd could persist. *Watch her throw ice sticks!* Franco planned to pass out on the couch. But watching the movie reflect off his daughter's eyes... he got out of his slouch. Held her tight. As they watched the princess. *Stop playing so nice. And start throwing ice.* The girl finally allowed to let loose out in the wild. Release all her rage. Well. Franco had his own wild. It was called *the cage...*

Franco sprouted up in the middle of The Garden.

Like a sunflower in the middle of a garden.

The sunflower blew into his corner.

Blew the standing fans' minds– Holding their heads. Launching high fives.

Franco could barely sit up in his corner. But he had survived the round four bell. He had survived. A round in Hell.

"Do you hear me, Franco? Can you see me?"

Franco's flooded eyes afforded a blurry view of... *Nina* before him. Head coach to her left. But Franco kept that to himself. As he caught his breath... "Look good, Brazil." Franco's frozen mouth cracked the slightest of smiles.

The fight team shared excited looks... *Franco's with it. He's with us...*

"What do we say to start every day?" Nina gave their guy a break and answered for him. "Beginner's mindset. Assume you know nothing. Learn everything."

Franco nodded as he wheezed–

"Forget it," commanded Nina.

The gutted fighter let out a guttural sound. *"Dafuh..."*

"For this one round. *You've done the work.* I want you to call on... *all of it.* With that *other* half a mind we know you

207

have."

The ref made his way around. *Time for the final round...*

But not before Joey Yo amped up his bro...

"Listen I know you're all banged up. But that fuck couldn't even *fuck* for 25 minutes!" Joey jabbed his finger at Umar. "And he's gonna roll with Franco—*The Bunns Lane Brawler*—for 25 minutes? *He's* wheezin. *He's* gassed. Like Herc after a jerkoff—"

"Thank you for those words, Joey," interjected Brazil with his hands in prayer form. Then pulled Franco aside for some final ones...

"Over at my academy, you call me a master. But in here... *you're the master.*" Brazil put his finger to Franco's forehead. "And you're the master of this. Now let's... *GET IT!*"

Franco danced around the canvas. Like the drunkest guy at a wedding.

Basayev more than happy to dance around with him. *Impossible* for Umar to lose by decision. So Franco laying off? *Hah! Stupid decision!*

The cageside commentators concurred...

"Whether he's gassed or not. Franco *must* get after it."

"No man stumblin around like that up to anything good."

As Franco staggered around, taking a mindful minute, he caught a glimpse of the provincial pasha...

Rulan Devmadov. The ruler who'd found the perfect man. To bring glory to his land. Umar "The Beast" Basayev. While most of the globe was using the fight game for good, Devmadov had made the fight game the public face of his fierce regime. Men only. In the cage *and* the crowds. And free tickets! To the only show in town. The one of mismatched beatdowns. Followed by pledging allegiance to the crown.

Then to the only party in town. Off the record of course. For top brass only of course. And The Beast of course. Oh. And underage girls of course. The story that had sparked the investigation. A 15-year-old girl roofied. Pushed off a roof. *What? There was no foul play. There was no proof!* The final ruling made by Rulan himself.

Franco swore that he if ever found T's attacker... *He'd fucking kill him.* Well in the meantime. *Basayev would be a nice fill-in...*

Franco sized up Umar and shot–

And–

Was easily stopped.

As the clock tick tocked...

Way to go, Franco. Nice mindful minute. Fuckin dummy. You took three!

The two-minute warning. Franco backed up to his own end zone. Looking across the line of scrimmage. *As hopeless as that 199th pick. That kid the size of a stick. Until. He squatted rack after rack. Took snap after snap. Audibled out of sack after sack. The SB MVP in '02. And just a few months back.* But...

The sure-footed linebacker looking right back... This Butkus-Baryshnikov...

That's it. That's how Franco could make the wheels come off...

"Ballet uh? 'Color's your tutu?'" managed the mangled fighter. The question wouldn't've bothered Franco personally. He could only imagine after all his mindful yoga that ballet was a beast. But he figured it'd chap Umar's ass worse than ass-less chaps. Yeah the man from somewhere near Bohemia now in the rap city... surely *hated* "Bohemian Rhapsody." Musta been driven wild. By "No Church in the Wild." If it was up to The Beast and his brethren, they'd take all the Freddy Mercurys. All the Frank Oceans. Ship em off to Mercury. Throw em in the ocean...

209

Yeah the kid from the streets just found the secret potion...

Franco had popped the cork and was now watchin Basayev uncork. All because of, *What color's your tutu?* It drove The Beast cuckoo! Charging like he was an apartheid supporter and Franco was Tutu.

Basayev uncorked harder than ever. Allowing Franco to pull a lever– One that Coach Nelly taught the broken-handed fighter long ago. *Bigger guy. Forget the Gable grip. Just take one leg. With one hand. One wrist.*

Followed by a twist...

Followed by...

Umar smashing to the mat!

The Nelsons exploding with claps...

But.

That wasn't that.

Franco just couldn't keep Basayev on his back. Brazil's Jiu-Jitsu had already worked its miracles.

Franco's only out... was a knockout. *Of a guy who'd never been knocked out...*

But. The five full rounds. The ballet putdown. The Nelly-styled takedown. It all had the big man wheezing... Steaming...

Gone all-Butkus as he resumed the beating...

Franco covered to a shell. Back in Hell. Toasting.

Basayev *laughing.* Like Jeff Ross giving a roasting.

And worse yet. Franco's blurred vision had...

Basayev... *growing...*

His hair growing out...

Until he looked like one person and one person only...

Terrible. Fuckin. Tony. "What are you the only asshole around here that gets a mindful minute? Mind if I have one for a minute?"

This was it. The fight's final minute...

"You suckered me back on Bunns Lane. You don't think

I can hit?"

BOOM! Terrible Tony laid a jab on Franco the felt like a haymaker from Tyson.

"That was cute last round. Thinkin of Kyd, Kyd, Kyd. Well you've got another kid, kid, kid–"

"*I know!*" Franco meant it as a roar... but it came out as a moan. Same for the jab he'd thrown...

"You have a talk with him one time? And you're a fuckin hero all the sudden? All these years he's been sufferin!" BOOM! A power shot that knocked Franco's lights out. For a split second. Like his house during Hurricane Sandy. His house that went dark a minute later...

"*Diswifi...*" moaned Franco. As he threw broken-hand jab after broken-hand jab. Like that sad-ass one-armed man. In that Springsteen song. Franco the Fighter now "The Wrestler." Crying. "*Diswifi...*" Over and over. Throwing that broken hand. Over and over...

No one in The Garden knowing...

What the poor man was moaning...

"*Diswifi...*"

No one. Except his son.

The one who told little sis to his right...

"He's yelling... *This is why I fight.*"

It was his way of communicating. Of setting an example. Of being. T could feel it in every fiber of his being. Wrinkling his brain. Inflating his heart. Fuck. It infected every part. Tingling from his neck to his toes...

And that's when T rose...

Junior hopped the security fence like Senior hopping a cage. Shouted at the edge of the stage–

"*LET'S! GO!*"

To the man. Still throwin that jab. That broken hand. Numb with pain. As its owner. Recalled Bunns Lane.

Recalled them taller, older, darker boys on the ball courts.
Seven-year-old Franco and his ankle-long shorts. A bully
pushin the little guy. To the point he almost cried. Until one
of them other taller, older, darker boys took him aside.
Taught Little Franco the ole high-low. *When he blocks high. You
blast him low.* Last that bully ever bothered Franco. As for
Franco's teacher. Where was he? *In his corner. Still teachin him...*

Franco glanced Brazil with the briefest of looks–

Then unleashed. A devastating hook–

A power left that reverberated the big man's abdo. Just
below his elbows. *Greetings from Joe.*

"What a shot! He's rocked!" The Force palmed Blount's
bald head. "The Beast now retaliating on instinct!"

"A world-class star. Gone WorldStar..."

Franco's opponent caromed off the cage.

Charged in red-eyed rage...

Then had to smile...

As the old man recoiled...

Saw Taz n Ray at the fence–

Shared their two cents–

Franco's recoil rounded into a roundhouse–

Into the belly of The Beast.

The Beast looked down... Saw Franco's foot stuck. A
moment in his mind forever stuck. That moment he realized.
He was completely fucked.

Cuz when you can't breathe...

You can't breathe.

The Beast dropped to his knees.

And like he was wearing one of them heavy cylinder caps
himself...

He tipped and planted.

Into The Garden.

Franco stood over him like Ali over Liston...

212

That Garden crowd... *Listen...*

The turned-up lights from above... *glistened.*

Franco fell into The Force. Grasped the mic... between gasps... *"T...J..."* Franco couldn't see where T was. He was blinded by the light. Like he was Young Springsteen. "Blinded by the Light."

"T...J..." Franco moaned. Followed by something unintelligible...

But TJ heard it. As if it was legible:

Go! Go to your show! Get after it! Go!

TJ nodded as he backpedaled. And pointed. To Franco's chest. Then his own. Then turned. To chase dreams of his own.

Franco finally caught a glimpse–

His son running through The Garden–

The old man wiped tears with his broken hand. Watching his son go. Like the kid's favorite book from long ago. *Oh, The Places You'll Go!*

Franco spotted Julie and Kyd through the haze of his hazels. Put his gloved hands to his heart...

Grace Nelson doing the same...

The Bogans twins throwing combos like that day Franco picked them up. Throwing combos like... Franco just threw in the cage.

The delirious fighter's vision ranged from that Rangers banner...

Over to a retired jersey. One that gave goose bumps. To the kid from Jersey. And the Piano Man's number... *12. Just like Tom Terrific.* Franco couldn't hear anything as he soaked in that singular moment. It's tone... *terrific.* Tonio Franco. On some Tone Terrific.

Franco raised his left fist. To return The Garden love felt. Then fell into his team. His face full of welts.

213

As Brazil held it high.
The Belt.

TRACK 21. NIGHT & DAY

THE AMBULANCE CRUISED THROUGH THE VILLAGE. Carrying Franco like *Die Hard* Bruce Willis. Bobbling his head like a Jeter bobblehead.

Franco peered out at the panorama of city lights. *Maybe he should go... Catch that show...*

The laid-up fighter shook his head. The one that musta got hit too many times. He was headed to the hospital after all. But what the hell... Why'd he keep hearin Dave Chappelle? *I'm Rick James, bitch!* Rick James who once said, *Cocaine is a hell of a drug.* Well. So is morphine. Inflating the fighter's mind. The fighter seeing in the window's slight reflection that his face was much improved. The locker room cuts to drain the blood. The stitches. The clean-up. Cold presses. The aviators Joey threw over Franco's elephantiasis eyes. When Joey told him—Joey who was always making comparisons to Maximus n Hercules—*Ya know, you look just like Freddy Mercury.*

"Any of you know that old club? Chester's?"

The young EMTs shook their heads.

But the old doc docked his specs—

"I saw Bruce there. Summer of '74."

"Ah missed it. Busy bein born."

"Well. First things first."

"It's around here ain't it?"

The doc peeked out the rear windows. "Two more blocks. Then a couple down Broad." The practitioner pointing which way.

Franco managed a nod in the bouncing ambulance. The bouncing ambulance that flamed up the swelling. But. *That even stronger feeling swelling...*

As the doc made his way to one bedside...

Franco darted out the other side—

Castling the doc like a king n a rook—

As Franco broke out of the ambulance—

And started to book!

The fighter threw his hood up and beat feet down the New York City street. The hooded, shaded bomber. Lookin like the Unabomber.

Franco made it the couple blocks—

Then almost got clocked—

"BACK THE FUCK UP, YO!" The six-five bouncer's arms flexed. Then he came correct— "Whoa! Francooo! I just saw you win, yo!"

"Ain't you workin?"

"Twitter, yo!" replied the big poppa who looked like Big Poppa. "What the fuck is you doin here, nigga!"

"My son's in the show."

"XBlacK?"

"Nah... *Gemini.*"

"Oh with that Dragon nigga. Talkin about Woodbridge... Hoboken... all kinda Jersey shit."

"Oh it's some shit."

"Let's ride."

As the big poppa showed the champ in...

The ambulance passed. Sirens blarin...

The shaded fighter was just another face in the crowd. The one roaring so loud. And sure, it was just a college night full of college acts. In a club on its last act. But the surrounding posters of artists from their early days. When they took the stage... Gillespie. *Sinatra.* Joplin. Dylan. Hendrix. *The Boss.* Whitney. *Biggie. Jay. Gaga.* Franco was dizzy by the time he got back to Dizzy.

The afro'd emcee meanwhile told them all to keep their hands high. "For Geminiiii!"

The red-frohawked Dragon ran a beat from the stage booth as—

TJ darted out. Wearing the same thing that man in the back was wearing. A Woodbridge hoodie. An oldie but goodie. As the pacing, crawling, crouching kid... hit em all with a newie...

"Oooh
Senior actin like a fresh-man
Poppin pills n Lite cans
Breakin phones n date plans
Oooh
That boy he rude he fresh man

Damn.
Need a whole new game plan
Some Curry slash n swish man
Oooh
That boy he dope he fresh man

Playin so hard
They gotta retire that jersey
I'm sayin bye-bye Gemini
Call me Young Jersey"

College kids vibing, bouncing, hands up...

As Young J spied Ray with Lenore. Back in the day, all down the shore. On endless summer nights. Like the one... where Lenore became T's first. So how could she... be the worst? Maybe T was just... *jealous*. Like that Jersey boy Jonas singin "Jealous."

Young Jersey slapped five with Lenore. And all his old pals from The Wood. There to see what's good. *And vibing like their boy was the truth...*

As he moved on to Candi. To Ruth...

The redhead in the blue jeans front and center. Vibing like her night couldn't have gone better. After all, her crowd included...

Both Sori and G! Both with their... *hands up for T??*

And Anders! Mouthing a... *sorry to T??* Well then fuck it. Young Jersey vibed with a point to all three.

"Fresh for my good girl hood girl
Like she from The Wood girl
Lay up on her couch curled
Strum away at her curls
Cuz I...
Know I...
Got the right girl
One that worth the fight girl
Handle herself nice girl
Bubbly as a Sprite girl

Overcome her plight girl
I could list all night girl"

And when Young Jersey finished his flow...
That girl joined the show.
Kimura. On-stage...
Blowing away that man in the shades...
Her golden glow under the lights. As her feet bopped in shelltops. Her tight jeans and a baby T. A sight as beautiful as Baby T.

The one Dad had heard about from Julie...
The one with her hair all teased.
As the crowd she teased–

"Yeah it's the TA
With the T & A
Your emcees T & K
Fuck a B we an A
Meant to be like P & J
Like me is B & he is Jay
Worked this rhyme out yesterday
So I could live my best today"

Young Jersey almost dropped his own mic. As he pointed at Kimura. She now the shark. He the remora.

As that sunglassed face in the crowd pointed as well. From his chest. To Young Jersey's. That hard-ass rapper on stage all misty-eyed.

Till he joined those golden eyes.
To sing some co-written lines...

"Not a rider
I'm driver..."

TJ and Kamara lay on the couch the next morning. Yeah her bed was bigger. But the grads wanted one last night on the couch. *Ya know, the LOVEseat,* T joked.

T who was now awake.

The sun cracking the drape.

It was around ten when she officially woke up.

Nestled under his arm, she spoke up–

"Why do you like stroking it?"

"What? Is that some kind of sick psychobiology question?"

"My hair." Kamara shook her head. "Frat boy."

Oh. Yeah. He'd been strumming a few strands. For a few hours.

"It's so frizzy..." continued Kamara.

"But..." TJ shrugged. "...it's yours."

Her goldens looked up at him. "They say when people see someone they're in love with, their eyes dilate."

"Oh yeah? Does anything else dilate?"

The loving– the joking– killed by a phone call–

TJ grabbed his cell. "What the... It's Mitch."

TJ emerged from the sinkhole that was the old couch.

Kamara watched as the boy in boxer-briefs kept it brief...

T then took a seat beside her. "That merger I did all the dirty work for..."

Kamara sat up as T continued...

"It went through. The firm made so much money on it... they can open a spot for another analyst." TJ exhaled breath held all year.

"Yay," Kamara said with a little clap. Then clocked T's scrunched brow. "What's the matter?"

"Our summer plans..."

Kamara had let T know. After the show. She was going to grad school at UC Redondo Beach. To which TJ replied, *Redondo Beach? Is that like, by AC?* To which Kamara replied, *It's like, by LA.* And she had to be there asap for a summer research study. Then she... invited T. *LA has anything you'd want to get into. Music. Business. Education. Oh. And sun. Lots and lots of sun...*

TJ had really appreciated that one. Fuckin interviewer and his fuckin, *Err New York has 39 nice days, not 40...* Meanwhile, TJ in LA with his shorty? Probably wouldn't regret that when he's 40...

Ah but reality bites. TJ sittin there like Ben Stiller in *Reality Bites...*

Kamara trying to find some light... "Come out before you start... Take long weekends... Work remote..."

"I'll have to start soon too... I'm not gonna have a day off till like... Thanksgiving. Like not Saturdays or Sundays. *Nothing,*" began the investment banker-to-be. "But it's like... ridiculous money. Like... rich by the time I'm 30."

Kamara took a breath. Her eyes gone as big as the roadblock before them. "Well, if it's what you want..."

The couched kid's elbows dug into his knees.

Topless yet a hundred degrees...

"I mean, I've worked the last four years for this. It'd be silly to say no now..."

"Yeah. No, you're right." Kamara exhaled. Hugged herself in the morning chill.

TJ hunched even further over. Like he'd just turned a hundred years older. With the realization... *they were over.* The realization... that this job ran all they way to the horizon. He'd have to cancel all other plans. Like they were fuckin Verizon. "Promise me you'll keep singing."

"What? What about... *you.*"

"You'll have the time..."

Kamara's eyes of gold watered. Like she was '64 Goldwater.

"You've really got something–" continued T.

"So do you–" cut Kamara. "So do w–" her crying cutting her off. *Fucking TJ. Cutting them off!*

"Yeah I've got something. Student loans," concluded T. He went to wipe away a tear–

But she brushed him away. Let them flow.

Some time later.

T headed home.

As TJ walked out of Kamara's brownstone into the rest of his life...

Franco was at his childhood home. *To say goodbye for life...*

Franco stood at the entryway. On the sunny Sunday. The restored place looking like it did decades ago. *He could see his old man sittin right there.* At the old olive table. Lit cig dangling. Smoke swirling up. Condensation running down his cracked Coors Light. The old man holding the paper folded into reading position. But sitting... with an unusual disposition. He was usually all pissed off as he perused the news. But that morning. The forty-something shouted to the high school senior at the door. "Look at this. A Franco made the paper. And it ain't the crime report!"

"What's it say?" the handsome kid asked.

"Triple double!" His old man laughed. Smacked the paper like it was a winning lottery ticket. "How bout that!"

The shrugging senior point guard hadn't even checked the stats after the game...

"Ten points. Ten rebounds. Ten assists," informed his old man.

The kid grinned. He'd gotten it done, didn't he? "Team was shootin a lot of threes. Lot of long rebounds."

"Bulllshit. I taught your ass," his old man began. "I taught your ass to get in there." His old man who used to walk the little boy up Bunns Lane. Put him on the court with all those other boys. Taller. Older. Darker. The old man tellin him, *Come on Franco. Get your ass in there.*

Franco. Arriving at his first martial arts lessons. At his first fight. Fingers interlocked in the fence. Half a mind to run away and never look back. Till he told himself. *Come on Franco. Get your ass in there.* And the most important people in his life. How many times did he almost shy away from all of em? Until he told himself. *Come on Franco. Get your ass in there.*

As Young Franco smiled over his old man's amusement...

Old Franco cried. *Over his old man. His Navy infantry old man. Who saw bombs in Vietnam. His Navy infantry old man. Who'd become lost at sea. But he'd kept their apartment shipshape. Didn't he.*

Old Franco wiped away tears. Took one last look at his old apartment. Restored to the same way. As it was back in the day.

Franco closed the door. His hand shook as he locked it for the last time. With that rusted Yankee key. The one stuck once again. The one his old man gave him for his 13th birthday. *Ya know what to do if it gets stuck?* Then off the boy's look– *Give it a yankee.*

Old Franco laughed out some last tears.

Then gave it a yankee...

And pocketed the key.

"Go 'head," the champ said to the hard-nosed man in the hard hat.

Franco walked away. Hands in his hoodie pockets.

223

Hearing "Wrecking Ball." As his old apartment. Got smashed by a wrecking ball.

Franco strolled past his old ball courts. Past a kid in ankle-long shorts. Working over n over on a crossover. "Nice work. Keep it up."

The little kid cracked a smile.

His top front teeth missing.

Just like the second floor.

Of the apartment behind him.

TRACK 22. SUNSET

THE SUN WAS SETTING SOMEWHERE WAY
BEHIND T.

T in his black Mustang headed toward the black tunnel.
Birthday drinks with Mitch. One last hurrah. Before T
became his bitch.

TJ had spent the day in Branchton. Followed by one final
stop at the DOG house. To clear the last of his things out.
Now chucked in his backseat freestyle. As he listened to
"Backseat Freestyle." The driver hitting himself in the head
over the misleading ditty. From Kamara's favorite album–*good
kid, m.A.A.d city*. The bop in the forehead once and for all
cementing it. *Oh, Kendrick's not celebrating the street life. He's
transcending it.*

The realization now as concrete as the concrete walls
closing in on T...

Cars headed the other way racing away...

T's Mustang funneling toward the tunnel.

And as its crawling wheels turned...

So did the ones in T's head...

How many people take this tunnel every day? Building better lives for themselves. Their families. Jersey locals connected to the wealth of the world. By this tunnel. This tunnel that's turned countless nobodies into somebodies. Somebodies who take this ride day in. Day out. Week in. Week out. So admirable. So why did T... want out? Why did he want to scream? To shout?

And this time... not out of rage. But out of that other feeling. That one he just couldn't shove. T was... *talkin bout love.* Like he was Jimmy Page. Ready to turn a new page. But. He was as planted as Robert Plant. Headed for a hole the size of a lead zeppelin...

TJ couldn't turn around. He'd be a fool to say goodbye to all that gold. But. What if all that glitters... *These thoughts... givin him jitters...*

Enough! T's mind was made up. He was going for gold. And not to be greedy... but he wanted two pieces.

The driver threw his hands out. Made two peaces.

The Mustang broke like a wild mustang– U-turning–
Crushing traffic cones–

It's driver screaming, *"I love gollld!"*[17]

The Mustang now rocketing off with Godspeed...

Like that robot toward a new destiny...

Because you are...
Who you choose to be.

The warm wind flew through T's hair as thoughts flew through his head. *No he wasn't throwing it all away. He'd continue to build. Just... in LA!* And all his worrying about taking care of Kyd... *Their father was Franco, kid!* And they'd all agree her best parent was the other. So take it easy big brother! *And show lil*

---

[17] T def remembers. To shout out *Goldmember.*

sis... how to get after it...

The driver sailed out of Sinatra's hometown so high after so much strife. The driver sailed out of Sinatra's hometown. Playing "That's Life."

TJ gave Hoboken one last look in the rearview as the Mustang blazed down the highway. As the track changed. To "My Way."

The driver no longer in a rut as he trucked past Rutgers. Last time, his mind jumping from Schiano. To Paterno. To Sandusky. Kid's mind all dusty. But T could see clearly now. The rain was gone.[18] *Everyone on Schiano's back. An assistant who says he never knew. And according to the worst reports, reported it. Shit could get so distorted— It's sick. Like the monster that caused the whole shit show. But as for Schiano? T'd be hard-pressed to find a man better. And he's only made a thousand better. The man is a state treasure!*

The Mustang fired past Rutgers. As T was fired up but far from annoyed. Remembering C Vivian Stringer. Carli Lloyd.

The driver inhaled the Garden State in-bloom. Now on some Jersey girl Judy Blume. Remembering when he was a little squirt, a nothing. Reading *Tales of a Fourth Grade Nothing.*

Then fifth grade. Learning about Washington crossing the Delaware...

The suspended bridge up ahead there...

Not long ago, TJ wouldn't dare...

But as the kid from Woodbridge...

Crossed the Delaware Memorial Bridge...

He had a perfect memory.

Of the day he left Jersey.

TJ took a last look back at the Garden State and all its green. And the boats in the Delaware... *what a scene.* The birthday boy who never. In a million years ever. Would think

---

[18] Over his past on some Johnny Nash.

227

leaving Jersey. Would be the best present ever.

Ah but inside. The two would never part.

TJ patted his chest twice. Banged Jersey into his heart.

From somewhere high in the air. If anyone was up there.
Up in the sky so bluuue. They would see it mooove...

The tiny black car.

Racing toward the sun.

Racing not to become.

A raisin in the sun.

A tiny black ant.

Crawling through endless farmland.

A small but mighty creature...

Escorting a lone dancer at the grand cotillion.

A one in seven billion.

A tiny dancer.

Off to find his "Tiny Dancer."

And up close...

Oh how the Mustang bombed.

As TJ.

Ran Elton John.

While deep in the heart of Woodbridge...

Franco was keepin it real. Like *real* fuckin real. Visitin his
old man. With Kyd on hand...

The two on a hilltop.

Lookin down at the rock:

MARCO FRANCO. 1950 - 1999. Veteran. Old Man.

Franco smiled... *Old Marco had insisted on two things. As he scratched his head on his deathbed. First, that his tombstone would say, "Old Man." Second, he didn't wanna live till Y2K anyway. World's gonna go to hell! he'd say.*

"Ay now I got a couple things to insist on."

Franco took a knee. "One. I wanna have that drink with ya." Franco took a bottle of Jack from his hoodie pocket. The tiny one he jacked from his last flight.

Franco took down his half of the shot. "Thought we could both cut back." Then left the little bottle at the base of the tombstone. Pulled Kyd in. "Two. Meet your granddaughter. Guess she should call you... her *old-old man.*"

Kyd toothpicked a tiny American flag next to the Jack. Then took a step back. Took it all in. As her curls danced in the wind... "What was he like?"

Franco took a breath from Mother Earth's surrounding hills. Surrounded yet by the steel cage of bridges and refineries that is rust-belt Jersey. "He was... Big. Loud. But... Sensitive. Funny."

"He sounds like you."

Franco's laugh belt across the rust belt. Of all the jokers he'd ever met on the streets of Jersey. It was his daughter. At the grave of his dead dad. That gave him the biggest laugh. He ever had.

Franco walked away hearing "Moment of Clarity." And like Jay, thanked God for granting him his. As he strolled off. With a hand around Kyd's.

TJ thought he'd catch her at her condo in Redondo. Or sippin her mimosa in Hermosa.

But nah.

He found her on Sunset. Rooftop. Whiskey on Sunset. Like those two lovers. *Before Sunset.* The girl rocking some set. The crowd spilling tequila sunsets. The bar manager not upset. The young girl rocking the old bar a welcome upset.

That's when Kamara saw him. Walking in at sunset. Her hon set. To sing with her on Sunset.

They sang well past sunset...

"Not a rider
I'm a driver
Pain my driver
I'ma I'ma thriverrr..."

TJ & Kamara together. An in-unison croon.
Two wolves. Howling at the moon.

ABOUT THE AUTHOR

Tom grew up in Jersey. On streets that show no mercy. Like the sun on a Hershey. Then he got a degree. Magna cum laude. From Rutgers. University.

After college, Tom worked in NYC. As an Analyst and Assistant VP. But had to flee. Apply his creativity—

At the UCLA School of Theater, Film and TV. Where Tom earned a Master's degree. Then wrote for Sony and Disney. Turned pitches into screenplays. He writes novels these days.

Tom's also busy leading his tutoring organization. Educating the next generation.

Tom otherwise spends time with his wife Tammi. Their kids. And friends & family. Whether that be on a sunny South Bay day. Or a trip. To NJ.

THE NUTSHELL

Two Tonio Francos. TJ and Franco. One on a stage. One in a cage. Both in a rage.

TJ. Falling for Kamara Day. On a college campus gone cray. The seniors caught in the culture war crossfire. TJ himself on fire. Burning in five different directions like he's all of One Direction. Big brother to Kyd. Fraternity VP. Intern in NYC. Rappin to Drag's beats. And. That f***ing demon he can't defeat. The one pushing him to the ledge. At Jersey's northeastern edge. Hoboken. The kid about to jump. No jokin. Haunted by many things. Especially THE Thing. Seven years lingering. Infecting. Tingling. Battling that other force. That one that makes him come alive. When he sees the girl with the golden eyes...

Kamara Day. The hipster scene queen. Her conscience clean. Already sorted through her childhood drama. No longer bothered by her father. No longer mixed up about her mixed race. But. Those dates with TJ in the moonlight. The choir girl dreaming of the limelight. Of singing as he rhymes tight. Assuming the spring lovers can weather the bad weather. Cuz sometimes it can rain all day. In NJ.

And right alongside the drama of the seniors... that of Franco Senior's. The retired MMA champ living with Julie and their six-year-old kid named Kyd. Somewhere in the woods of Jersey. Yet still stompin in his old stomping grounds. Running the family fight club in Woodbridge. His up-and-comer's upcoming match a bridge. To sponsors who could keep the club afloat. Or. The Francos go broke. Lose everything they own. Extra motivation for Franco to reclaim the throne. As he battles. A demon of his own.